Ulterior Motives

ULTERIOR MOTIVES

A Novel by

Fla'She

IamFlaShe Publishing, LLC

Published by IamFlaShe Publishing, LLC

Front and Back Cover Design by Je' Designs Graphx
Back Cover Photo by Dell Photography
Edited by Christina Brown

To submit questions, comments, or concerns about this
book or for information about bulk purchase discounts,
please send an email to:
iamflashe12@gmail.com
Or visit www.everythingflashe.com or
www.flashespeaks.com

DEDICATION

$\mathscr{I}$ dedicate this book to all those who have experienced domestic violence or some form of abuse. May God give you the strength and courage you need to walk away and direct you towards the path of fulfilling your life's destiny.

Acknowledgments

God you know my fears, my personal weaknesses, and my sins, yet you have blessed me with talents and the strength to use them. I can't thank you enough for guiding me through it. I love you for never leaving me during those moments I felt I couldn't do it. Momma thanks for being tough on me. I guess that's your way of uplifting me; and well it worked. To my friends, family, and fans thank you for supporting me over the last five years. Your positive feedback and reviews have inspired me to complete this novel.

Love Sick

Jacksonia "Sonia" Bradshaw

A splatter of blood flew from my mouth just before falling to the cold cement floor. The perpetual blows to my face that I endured within the first few minutes of his return were unbearable. His fists were enormous and I couldn't understand how he could comminate me like that especially with our baby boy in the next room. The physical and emotional damage at this point is just irrevocable. Due to the increase in Terrence's alcohol and drug use, his physical and verbal abuse towards me has spun completely out of control. I held my mouth in disbelief and frustration. I could no longer hide the pain I'd been keeping from our friends and family. It was time for us to get someone to intervene in our relationship and fix our chaos filled home before we exchange vows next month. I was weak, emotional, and helpless. My Dear Terrance, my Ter-bear, my fiancé, my heart beat had changed in only a matter of months. His sickness had taken over his mind, body, and spirit in its entirety. It feels like he's grown more difficult to deal with since recovering from prostate cancer. I thought to myself, "I really need this girl's getaway." Terrence spoke to me out of anger immediately interrupting my thoughts.

"Ask me where I've been again and see if I don't sock your pathetic ass in the mouth one more time stupid bitch!" He yelled out. Terrence smelled of booze and women's perfume. I laid across the firm bathroom floor trying to plead with him.

"Baby you're misinterpreting my words. I was worried sick about you! You didn't take your bag of medication with you and I wanted you to be okay." I told him. Whenever he would use cocaine and drink he would come home and take whatever issues he has with himself out on me.

"Fuck you and that medication!" He said abruptly. I began wailing uncontrollably.

"How can you speak to me in such an inappropriate way when I have always been there to lift you up at your lowest? I was the only one there for you this entire time; the only one!" I screamed. Terrence looked at me as if I disgusted him then grabbed me by my hair lifting me to my feet. He was sweating profusely. My body trembled as he looked me straight in my eyes and told me I wasn't shit to him anymore. My lips quivered as I attempted to speak. "Our son can hear you! It isn't healthy for him! He's only three years old." I said. Our baby began kicking and screaming from behind the closed door.

"Mommy! Mommy! Are you okay?" I heard our offspring scream out. Terrence shut the bedroom door leaving Jaxon all alone in the living room.

"You're frightening him Terrence!" I warned him.

"Take off your fucking clothes and suck my dick!" He demanded.

"Really? I am not doing anything sexual with you while you're in this state of mind." I replied. He angrily shoved me against the wall hitting my head in the process.

"Put this monster down your throat hoe." He screamed just before slinging my fragile body into the glass door of the shower. With my face pressed against the glass I screamed for him to stop.

"No Terrence! Our baby is right outside our bedroom. Please stop!" I heard Jaxon crying out for me.

"Oh you want to worry about his punk ass crying? I'll give you both something to whine about." Suddenly Terrence pulled me down by my hair and dragged me across the bathroom and bedroom floor into the living room where our baby boy sat whimpering on the floor. Still holding on tight to my ponytail, Terrence picked me up from the floor and slung my body across the back of the microfiber sofa then ripped my panties off of me.

"No Terrence! No!" I desperately screamed. My baby began crying and screaming even louder. Terrence tore my robe completely from around my body leaving me exposed. "Don't do this in front of our baby T. Not in front of our baby." I begged. He unzipped his pants and I quickly turned my face away and closed my eyes. Tears fell down my face from the thought of what he wanted to do to me. "This could forever ruin us, our baby; our family!" I yelled out.

"Dumb, bitch! I wouldn't rape you in front of our son. Your sex isn't even worth it." He picked me up and threw me over the couch and I landed on my back right onto our glass coffee table. All I could do was lay there in pain screaming for my son to be okay. Terrence walked away leaving me naked on the living room floor with my body partially covered in blood. He opened the front door, walked out and slammed it shut. Jaxon ran over to me, falling into my arms. His little body was trembling as I held him close and told him that everything would be okay.

Positions of Interest

Kelis "Keke" Ryan

I adjusted my black floral blouse and my red leather pencil skirt before tapping on Principal Ford's door.

"Come on in Ms. Ryan," he said.

"You requested to see me, Sir?"

"Yes. Have a seat please." I sat down as quickly as I could so that I could return to my classroom for pre-planning. Judging by Principal Ford's facial expression, it seemed as if he had something very important to discuss with me.

"You look very exotic today Ms. Ryan." Principal Ford mentioned.

"Thanks." I responded. He leaned back in his reclining desk chair with his hands up to his mouth. "It has been brought to my attention that you do other work outside of teaching art for our school."

"Yes. That's correct." I told him. "A lady should have multiple incomes."

"I admire your ambition, and from my understanding this other position you hold is very different from what you do here at The Dallas School of Arts and Humanities," he said with a

14

smirk on his face. I gave him a blank stare without responding. "Ms. Ryan I just want to tell you that hiring you as the Director of Arts was definitely one of my greatest accomplishments thus far."

"Thank you and I appreciate this opportunity. I love what I do. However, with all due respect Principal Ford, I kind of have a very busy schedule today and I was hoping that this meeting or whatever you were planning to speak to me about would have been done briefly." Principal Ford stood up and locked the door of his office before returning to his seat.

"That's just it Ms. Ryan. I'm aware that this is your planning period and I was hoping that I could get some of your services during this time."

"What kind of services are you referring to?" I asked him out of curiosity. He crossed his arms as if he was becoming agitated with my nonchalant responses.

"Well, for starters, I was informed that the other services you offer outside of the classroom consist of adult activities. Is this information factual Ms. Ryan?"

I paused as I gathered my thoughts. 'Ha! If this man thinks I would even consider having his obese bald headed ass as a client he has another thing coming.' I uncrossed my legs and got up from my seat, walked over to his side of the desk, placed my knee in between his legs, pulled his tie towards me, and whispered in his ear, "You can't afford those services Principal Ford." I rubbed his white hairless head and walked right out of his office. When I walked back into my classroom I sighed and took a deep breath. This night job is becoming overwhelming. I have to develop a more exclusive clientele. It is not cute, safe, or professional having the two overlap. That was a close call. Although I absolutely love being an art director I have been considering resigning for a while. The independent dominatrix lifestyle is guaranteed more money, requires less time, and gives me the freedom to travel whenever and wherever I desire. 'We must plan this ladies trip soon. I need to get away and reflect on my career choices because lately, this city life has been extremely draining for me.' Immediately calm came over me because I knew I would see my friends and family in a few hours. It was my high school's 10 year class reunion and my plans were to see him; my ex. Although, I've exclusively dated women for the last eight years, I yearn for his tender familiar touch. Our high school experience together was undeniably exciting. He was the star quarterback and I was popular for my charisma, style, and beauty. As cheerleader captain, I got plenty of attention, as did he, but most importantly we enjoyed giving and receiving affection and quality time from one another. We were the youngest power couple and could have possibly been a great example to other young couples, had we remained strong. However, his position as a quarterback and as "Kelis Ryan's" boyfriend got him plenty of outside attention which lead to him cheating throughout the end of our relationship. Eventually it got old to me and I suddenly found myself being comforted by the arms of another woman. I was crazy about him and loved the shit out of 'our thing.' He was there for me whenever I needed him and I was there for him. I'm not trying to sound cliché' but I was literally the yin to his yang. On the contrary, I couldn't stand to be swindled since I could have had anyone I wanted. It sucked though, because I only wanted him.

After mingling and catching up at the reunion dance, I went back to my hotel room and waited patiently. I'd slipped him a note in his pocket before saying goodbye. The note read, "*Meet me in room 997 for a night cap.*" I showered and slipped on a black lace teddy and covered myself with a black satin robe. I tied my hair up in a messy bun and sipped my drink while flipping through Victoria Secret's latest catalog. Soon after refreshing and getting a bit more comfortable there were knocks at the door. My heart began to race and I noticed my hands sweating.

"Coming!" I yelled. I took a sip of my Patron on the rocks, one last glimpse in the mirror, and a deep breath before approaching the door. I opened the door and there he stood looking as nervous and anxious as me. He stepped into the room and gave me the warmest hug I'd ever gotten from him. Hmmm that scent was familiar but I couldn't put my finger on it.

"You smell nice." I told him. "What is that?"

"Don't tell me that you don't recognize the cologne that I'm wearing?" he asked staring right at me. He looked so damn sexy and I started to stutter over my words before answering.

"Wha- uh- yea- well of course I remember. It's Hugo by Hugo Boss!" I heard myself yell out almost showing too much excitement. He sat at the desk and I laid across the bed. "Would you like something to drink?" I asked.

"What are my options?" Devonte' asked.

"Patron, Ciroc, and Hennessey."

"You already know what's up Mango! Hennessey on the rocks…"

"Mango?" I laughed. "You haven't called me Mango in years!"

"Yeah well, I guess you can say I'm trying to make us feel comfortable." Devonte' said, reassuring me that he was concerned with me being okay with this.

"Thanks for being considerate." I poured his drink and brought it over to him then I sat on the desk right in front of him. He took a few sips of his Hennessey before speaking.

"Damn Mango, you still have some sexy ass legs."

"Thanks and you still have those sexy glistening eyes," I said blushing. He uncrossed my legs and moved his chair closer towards me.

"Come down," he said grabbing my hands. I slid down from the desk onto his lap straddling him. It felt good being in familiar arms. "Are you okay?"

"Yes I'm lovely." I wrapped my arms around his neck and he held on to my waist.

"I already know the fragrance you're wearing," he kissed me on my neck then whispered in my ear, "Magnetism."

"Yeah, that's what I'm wearing. You know exactly what you're doing to me right now, don't you?" He smiled a devilish grin while finishing his drink. Then he moved strands of my hair behind my ear and kissed me on my forehead; his signature kiss. Without warning, my legs began to shake. I looked directly into his eyes almost reaching his soul. "You miss me don't you?" I asked. Without answering he placed his hand on the nape of my neck and pulled my head toward his and our lips locked.

"Let me show you just how much I miss you." Devonte' stood up with my legs wrapped around his waist and sat me back onto the desk. With his hands moving underneath my dress, he pulled my panties down my thighs. Placing them to his nose before throwing them across the room, Devonte' smiled. "Hmmm, smells just like mangos." I giggled and blushed at his statement. That was the very reason he nicknamed me Mango.

"Come here." I told him aggressively. I pulled him by his arm and placed his hand near my treasure. "Come inside." He looked at me as if he'd won a prize. Inserting two fingers at a time without warning had me extremely turned on. Our tongues reunited passionately, and I took every sign of what he was expressing to heart. "Oh that feels so freaking good!" I attempted to moan quietly, but then he hit my spot and I let out a whimpering scream. "Fuck me harder Devonte.' That's right Baby, fuck me just like that!" I said throwing it back at him. "Don't stop there!" My treasure was crying for more of him. His penis bulged from his pants, and I hadn't seen anything like it in a very long time. The thought of him getting an erection because of me made me even hotter. He pulled his fingers out of me and put one in my mouth and the other in his. We tongue kissed each other while licking my cream from his fingers.

"You taste so damn good Mango. Don't you agree?" he stated sarcastically.

"Hell yeah," I whispered.

"Why are you whispering? Tell Daddy what's on your mind. I want to hear you. I came to give you whatever it is you need."

"Mango wants to be kissed." I told him. Without hesitation, Devonte' fell to his knees and gobbled my treasure box. He sucked on my clit effortlessly and I sincerely enjoyed every moment of his indulgence. I pulled his face closer and wrapped my legs firmly around his neck almost smothering him. He came up for air and kissed my lips. I looked down and noticed his penis fighting to be released from his pants. I massaged it while we kissed some more.

"Pull it out and beat it," he instructed while moving closer to me. I unzipped his jeans and pulled 'Soldier' out of hiding. I held it in my hands and stared at it before going to work. Devonte' moaned as I pleasured him. I had an instant desire to put it in my mouth so I hopped down from the desk and pushed him forcing him to sit back on the chair. I took my robe off and slipped my teddy down to my waist then I kneeled down in front of him. Gently caressing his dick up and down, I placed my entire mouth around it. I suckled on the head right before moving it to the top of my mouth. His warm and wet dick suddenly struck the back of my throat. I looked up at him with my eyes tearing and placed his hand around my bun. Lifting my head quickly, I told him to fuck my face. He partially hesitated just before taking control of the situation. I rubbed my clit with one hand and my right nipple with the other. I looked up only to see him biting his bottom lip with his eyes closed.

I mumbled, "Cum in my mouth, baby." He used both hands to pull me in closer to his body. It was something about deep throating that turned me on like never before. He fucked my face harder as I rubbed my clit. My treasure was talking back with every slippery wet noise. I felt an orgasm brewing and I wanted him to cum with me. I moved my mouth from his dick and started jacking him off.

"Cum all over my breasts, Daddy!" I screamed while rubbing my pussy faster and faster.

"Oh God, oh God, baby I'm about to release! I'm cumming for you, baby." Devonte' stood up as I was attempting to gather myself and came all over my erect breasts just as I'd requested.

Explosive

Savannah "Syn" Dominique

The sweat from Drake's balls submerged my face as he hovered over my relaxed body in an attempt to cum in my mouth. He stood there tall, dark, and handsome wearing nothing but a smile and his Timbs. He jacked-off right above my head as he gazed down at my nakedness. His enthusiasm to cum on my face forced my kegal muscles to contract. That strong, sexy man knew exactly how to please me in every way possible. Usually I would have asked him to make love to me first, but today I had something different in mind. It was our fourth Valentine's Day together and I wanted him to last as long as time permitted him to. (With black balloons floating throughout my apartment, red rose petals surrounding us, and tea light candles leading to the bathroom which lit up the room, I proposed a bet that I could swallow every ounce of semen that came from his penis in one sitting.) You see Drake wasn't your average guy. He would always produce enough cum to fill up at least a 6 oz glass. Most guys ejaculate about 1-2 teaspoons per ejaculation. I found it to be exciting and extremely sexy just to see his penis rise to the perfect height. Drake's penis was the kind every girl would dream of having. It curved to the right and was a perfect 9 ½ inches long and 3 inches wide. It was huge, but Drake was great at teaching an amateur, as I once was, how to handle it plus more.

He came straight over after working a 12-hour shift at the local detention center. Shortly after he walked through the door I stripped him naked. I on the other hand had taken a nice long bubble bath and decided to lie on my leather couch in my birthday suit with a bow around my neck until he arrived. Drake unlocked the front door and looked at me from head to toe.

"Well damn!" he said walking over to the couch where I laid stretched out for a kiss. "How are you, Sexy? How was your day?" Drake asked as I removed his shirt from his hard and ripped body.

"It was fine, handsome, but it's about to get better."

"Oh really?" he asked, "And why is that?" He looked around taking everything in at once. "Baby you did all this for me?"

"Yes! Of course I did. You deserve it. You work so hard which is why I'm going to do that thing we talked about a few days ago and you're going to love it!" I told him confidently.

"What? Take it up the ass or swallow my nut?" Drake asked smiling.

"You'll just have to wait and see Mr. Nasty."

While removing the last piece of clothing, I grabbed his arm and sat him down on the couch. His dick stood at attention before I could properly greet it with my mouth.

"Oh it looks like someone missed me more than you did." I said jokingly.

"That's not true, baby girl. I missed that ass of yours too!"

We both laughed as I kneeled down on the floor in front of him and whispered in his ear.

"I want you to fuck me like a slut and call me a bitch, but first I want you to beat your meat and nut in my mouth and I'll take care of the rest."

"Lay on the floor," he instructed.

I obeyed as he stood up from the couch and got right behind me. Watching him sling *Mandingo Warrior* back and forth made my body shiver. I was too anxious to see what was in store. I started to play with my clit when he began making obvious motions which alerted me that he was about to climax.

"Open your mouth! I'm about to nut, bitch!" Drake aggressively yelled before shoving his huge black dick down my throat. He knew I preferred to be handled in a rough manner and like always, he had given me precisely what I desired. I quickly stood up in an attempt to catch every drop of his juices with my tongue. I couldn't let any of that sweet nectar go to waste. With my back leaning against the couch, Drake choked the back of my neck and pulled me closer into his genitals. As I swallowed his entire cock he pinched my left nipple. He grabbed me by my shoulder pulling me to my feet. He then forced me to kneel on the couch face down with my ass up. I turned around to see what he was doing and his dick had risen like he hadn't just cum down my throat minutes ago. I waited anxiously for him to enter inside of me. It was an instant moment of bliss that controlled my body in every way possible. Daddy pulled my hair as I arched my back a little bit more before coming inside.

"Yesssss!" I screamed. "Drake baby you're so fucking deep! Shit! That's right, Daddy! Mmhhmm keep it right there! Fuck my pussy, baby! Fuck my pussy hard! That's right, baby! Mmmhhhmm keep it right there!" Drake smacked my ass and held on to my hair like it was attached to a saddle.

"You love this dick?" he asked.

"Yes I'm in love with it!" I yelled.

"Well act like it!" Drake commanded.

Drake spread my ass apart before digging deeper into my love.

"Deeper!" I screamed. "Uhn hmmm, deeper Daddy! Deeper!" I screamed while grinding my hips to the rhythm of his stroke. Drake knew how to please me. Never once did we ever make love and he not take real good care of me.

"Choke me, baby! I'm going to cum all over that big juicy dick! Is that what you want too, Daddy? Do you want me to cum all over it!?!" He smacked my ass before answering.

"Nah I'm going to bust all in that fat juicy pussy! Who is that pussy for, bitch?" he asked stroking me harder.

"You, baby! Nobody but you, Daddy!" It's all for you! I yelled. "Nobody but you! That's right, Daddy keep fucking me. Fuck! Uhn hmmm, baby I'm about to cum on that big fat dick!" I moved my hips faster. "Yessss I'm cummmmiiinnnggg!" My entire body trembled as I searched for a way to contain it.

He turned me around and slid his dick in my mouth.

"Taste your pussy! Tell me if that pussy taste good!"

"Mmhhmmm." I sucked all of my wetness from his testicles while moving my hand up and down the shaft of his penis in an attempt to make him cum too. He grew weak from the sucking noises and the stroking of my hand. Shortly after I felt the semen run down my throat almost choking me. He raised my head up and I continued to suck all of his juices as I swallowed every bit.

"Marry me, Savannah." Drake said as he came all over my body. His sticky cum juice laced my face, mouth, and chest. We both laid on the couch trying to catch our breath. I smiled at him before saying, "Yes. Of course I'll marry you."

CHAPTER 1

The Weekend Getaway

I'd been anticipating a quick getaway with my girls for a while now, but our schedules would always clash. And let's not get on deciding the perfect destination that best fit all three of us. Finally we agreed at the last minute to book a resort in the Bahamas instead of Jamaica or the cabins in North Georgia for our weekend escape. Jacksonia, whom we refer to as Sonia, and I haven't seen Kelis in what feels like ages since we both reside in Atlanta and Kelis in Dallas, TX. Kelis aka Keke is our fun, spontaneous, and wild lesbian friend from college who always knew how to get a party started. Although Sonia has a man and I'm still on the dating scene, I'd say she and I live very routine lives which in turn can be extremely boring at times. Unfortunately for me, getting a man in Hotlanta has been a drab since there are so many undercover gay brothers and the ones who aren't gay are already married. Even though it gets lonely at times, cosmetology school has been keeping me occupied. For some reason I've always attracted dogs, my ex fiancé Drake being one of them. That Negro had the audacity to ask me to marry him after getting not one, not two, but three females pregnant during our five year relationship. It's all good though because I played around a bit also while in undergrad, but it still sucks that I had to make the decision to give up the ring and his good loving. Sonia got lucky in the love department when she met her fiancé Terrence whom she'll be marrying next month. They have been through so much in the past couple of years as he was fighting prostate cancer at such an early age. Blessed with beauty, awesome bodies, and money, all of us graduated from Spellman together and are making the best out of our situations. Sonia is a botanist and Keke is an art director of a prestigious school and works as a professional dominatrix part-time. Yes, that's a job right up her alley. Since she's single, built like a stallion, and a very successful black woman, Keke's opportunity to participate in domineering acts made me kind of envious, but in a good way. I always knew, from the moment I first met her that she needed to do something in relation to sex. Sonia and I were more like undercover freaks in school and even more so undercover with professional reputations to uphold. However, being a mixed African American and Chinese woman, Sonia never had an issue finding anyone who viewed her otherwise. Most people's perceptions of her are that she's a good sweet and innocent girl from New Haven, Connecticut who isn't aware of her surroundings and any potential threat, but I beg to differ. Sonia knew enough and did enough in her past that could ruin her career as well as her expectations for her future family. The difference between us and Keke is that she never hid who she truly was. She did drugs here and there, slept around, wore her gay pride paraphernalia (which still makes me cringe), had wild hair, and her grades were horrible at times, but she always knew what to do to change that if you know what I mean...

"This is going to be fun ladies!" I told the girls over the phone as we browsed through the catalog of The Cove Atlantis in Paradise Island, Bahamas.

"Girl, they even offer unlimited alcoholic beverages with this all- inclusive package," Keke said in astonishment. "It's going to be a hell of a good weekend if you ask me!"

"Yes it is," I said agreeing.
Sonia hesitated before speaking.

"Well how is it that we have the option to drive to a secluded area which is only three and a half hours away from Atlanta, and still choose to spend an ironically crazy amount of money to sit on a beach and get sunburned?"

"Sonia, if you want to spend your weekend in the North Georgia mountains while Syn and I have a blazing time sitting on the beautiful sandy beaches in the Bahamas while sipping on mojito's then so be it! But, I'm here to tell you, regardless of what you decide, we're still going to the Bahamas!" Keke said partially frustrated.

"It's just that I don't want to be so far away from Terrence. He really needs me, and I can't be worried if something happens to him while I'm away."

"Sonia I understand your concern, well 'we' understand you're concerned with Terrence's health, but isn't the cancer in remission? And hasn't it been for the past year?"

"Yes Syn, but I'm just so worried he'll forget to take his meds or not eat at the appropriate time of day."

"Well let's not worry about that Sonia. If it helps any, I'll get your plane ticket and Keke and I will split the total cost of your trip. We will allow you additional time to talk it over with Terrence and you let us know your final decision by the end of the week."

"That's very generous of you Syn, but how are you going to volunteer Keke's money?"

"Because we discussed it when we initially started planning this trip and we've mutually agreed to split the bill since you two have been through so much and are planning a fabulous wedding that will be here before you know it." Keke assured Sonia.

"Ladies I'm thrilled and I truly appreciate your generosity and in the mean time I will discuss everything with my honey and get back to you by the end of the week."

"Okay sounds like a plan," I said.

"Talk to you soon Sonia! Don't forget what I said earlier! Be blessed doll." Keke said before disconnecting her line.

I thought to myself, "This is going to be one wild trip!" Let the fun begin.

CHAPTER 2

Vision of Paradise

We arrived at our long awaited destination Friday morning. The sun was bright and crisp which lead us to search through our handbags for our sunglasses. The taxi driver told us it had rained all week and spoke of how our beauty must have brought sun back onto the island. The scenic route that was taken from the airport to the resort was breathtaking. I'd never seen anything like it and from the looks on the girl's faces; I doubt they had either. We drove around a hill and were immediately awed by the gorgeous views of the ocean waters that sat below us. The sound of Bob Marley's "No Woman No Cry" graced our ears and prepared us for the vacation of our dreams.

"Have you lovely ladies been to the island before?"

"My fiancé and I won a trip here a couple of years ago through our local radio station, but due to his poor health we were unable to accept the invitation," Sonia explained to the cab driver.

"Well I have never won a trip or had the offer, but I'm here now and I plan to take full advantage of it," Keke stressed.

Fred looked through his rear view mirror as they spoke.

"You three beautiful ladies shouldn't have any problems enjoying your stay or finding the man of your dreams if you look closely," he expressed winking at us.

We all laughed before exiting the cab.

We'd definitely found paradise! Our resort was near other gorgeous resorts, but none of them had anything on what we were about to experience. It was a private sanctuary that sat on the very end of the island. We were surrounded by palm trees, the gorgeous ocean, and never before seen white sand. As we walked up to the entrance of our destination, we were greeted by two handsome half- dressed men who served us with smiles and the options of mango juice or mojitos. Of course we all opted for mojitos in an attempt to keep the vibe going. We were astounded by the amenities offered by the resort. Our mouths fell open when we entered the lobby which was filled with poker tables, slot machines, gorgeous chandeliers, an underground aquarium, and entrances to the spa, restaurants, and night clubs on the property. Finally arriving to our suite with an ocean view, we became even more enamored with the yellow rose petals leading from our front door to the double doors which lead to the outside balcony. The suite consisted of three bedrooms, three bathrooms, a full kitchen, and a bar.

"I really appreciate you ladies for giving me such an amazing opportunity to experience something this beautiful for the first time ever," Sonia said almost in tears.

"Aww Sonia, it's cool girl just sit back, relax, enjoy the view, the drinks, and all that God created for us to see," said Keke.

Sonia laid across the king size bed that was off from the kitchen. She appeared to have a lot on her mind, but was attempting to hide it with what she referred to as "happy tears." Keke and I looked at each other as if we mutually agreed there was more to her story.

"Well I'm going to lie down too girly, I'm tired."

"Okay, you two can relax, I have to get my workout in so that I can keep my abs right before damaging my liver over the next few days from indulging in all this alcohol." Keke said before going into the back of the resort to the room with the queen sized bed.

"Cool," I responded. As I was dozing off into my morning nap, I heard the door of our suite open and close. "Dang, Keke is serious about keeping her body in shape," I thought to myself.

CHAPTER 3

Up and Down

As Keke entered the elevator, she was unexpectedly greeted by a couple who was obviously getting it on. The lady, who was a young African American beauty was kneeling down on her knees with her sports bra up and her perky pierced nipples hanging from underneath. Her man, an older Caucasian guy who appeared to be in his late fifties, stood there smiling with his erect penis in her mouth.

"Oh don't mind us," the man said winking at her.

It came as no surprise to Keke who was damn near wet from the sight of things.

"It's okay, I understand. I don't mind watching. Do your thang girlfriend!" Keke responded as she looked up into the corners of the elevator to search for cameras. Fortunately there were no cameras to alert the front desk or security so they kept riding the elevators up and down from the sixth floor all the way to the twenty- first floor. Sista girl was going to town catching every bit of his secretions and every slurp of her own spit. She was definitely a swallower and wasn't ashamed to handle her business when it came down to pleasing her man. Keke was an obsessive self-pleaser, and before you knew it, she had unzipped her jacket exposing her hard nipples through her sports bra. She then licked her fingers and put them inside of her biker shorts. Keke began touching and teasing her clit moving in circular motions which was the quickest way she'd get herself off. The guy began to moan as the suckling noises from his ladies mouth chimed in with Keke's dampened pussy sounds as well as her sensual moans. He watched Keke's facial expressions and instructed his lady to play with herself also.

"That's right Rach, suck on Poppa," he said before bending his knees and grabbing her hair bringing her head closer towards him covering his entire penis with her mouth. "Suck Poppa's cock good!" He began grinding her face causing her to gag. She didn't mind it either because she loved to gag and was thrilled by Keke watching and somewhat participating. The old man sped up his pace and before he could warn his lady he was ejaculating down her throat. Keke screamed as she rubbed her clit faster and faster in an attempt to cum in unison with the couple.

"Yes! Yesss! I'm having an orgasm too Poppa!" Keke yelled out somewhat embarrassed. The couple looked over at her as they tried to catch their breath with a smirk on their faces just before dressing themselves.

"Hi I'm Rachel, and this is my husband Tony." Rachel reached out her hand to Keke for a handshake. Keke hesitated before shaking her hand.

"My apologies, I get kind of weak after an orgasm. I'm Keke, well my friends call me Keke, but my name is Kelis. It's very nice to have met you two." Keke smiled before shaking Rachel and Tony's hand. "By the way I practice S&M and I would absolutely love for you two to partake in a session. I'm here with my friends for the weekend. Anyway, I don't mean to ramble, so here's my card."

"It's okay sweetheart! We admire your openness. We get a rush when we make love in public places and we love voyeurs," Rachel admitted. They all laughed as if they were in cahoots to any freaky approach.

"Well that makes me feel more comfortable. How about we set up a session? The morning works for me if you're up to it. My fees are on my website which is at the bottom of the card. Feel free to email me and set up an appointment for whichever time works best for you." Rachel and Tony looked at each other and smiled.

"You're also assertive and business oriented. We admire that, especially in young people. Forget the rates. Pencil us in for 10:30 am and you can come to our luxury suite." Tony said.

"Wonderful!" Keke responded excitedly. "I'll see you in the morning and I'll send you an email confirmation after I'm done working out."

"Are you on your way to the fitness center?" Tony asked.

"Yes I have to make sure I stay in shape even on vacation." Keke said.

"It's beautiful. It's on the 15th floor and has a 360 degree panoramic view of the ocean," Rachel informed Keke.

"Sounds gorgeous! Thanks I will see you guys in the morning. Have a good evening."Keke told them.

"Have a good workout!" Tony said.

CHAPTER 4
Unraveled

Keke arrived back at our suite sweaty and anxiously waiting to shower.

"Are you almost done in there Syn?" she yelled out.

"Yes I'll be out shortly!" I told her. "There are two other restrooms you know. Maybe you should use one of those."

"Sonia just went into the other restroom with the shower and my restroom only has a bathtub."

"Well isn't that what you requested; a bathtub?" I said jokingly.

"Yes, but...never mind I'll wait. Just hurry up because I'm sweating out my hair." Keke mentioned out of frustration.

I stepped out of the shower and quickly snatched one of the towels that was hanging on the towel rack and wrapped my wet body with it, then grabbed my underwear before exiting the restroom.

"Thank you!" Keke said before slightly knocking my things out of my hand. I stood in the doorway preventing her from shutting the door on me and she started to run the shower then stripped naked right in front of me.

"So what are you in such a hurry for slut puppy?" I asked her.

"Huh? What are you talking about? I just finished working out and I needed to shower as quickly as possible because I'm hungry and don't want to go down for brunch all sweaty and raggedy looking."

"No, there's something else." I said shaking my head. "I can see that your aura is different. You had sex with someone didn't you?" I asked abruptly.

"Syn, why are you always going above and beyond when you jump to conclusions? I just finished a strenuous workout and I want to look my best and smell good while doing it. After all, we are on vacation. I could meet my future wife here and I need to be on point if I do." We both snickered.

"Well you know I think you should be looking for a husband anyway. The Bible says..."

"I know what the damn Bible says Syn!" She yelled cutting me off. "Let's not start with the sin thing this early in the day please. I've been having a lovely morning thus far and I will not let you and your strict religious beliefs steal my joy; at least not for the next 72 hours. Live a little! Find you a man first then maybe, just maybe I will consider it."

I sensed the irritation in her voice. "Okay, I'll leave you be for now, but you still need a man. A woman can't do anything for you. You're too damn independent and you love to fuck too often. Men love to fuck which is perfect for you."

"Listen, Savannah! I've dated Mr. Nympho, Mr. Wealthy, Mr. Intelligent, as well as Mr. Fine, and I don't want any of them," she stressed. "I just need you to live your own life and let me live mine. It's bad enough I have to hear it from my mother every time I speak to her. '*When are you going to give me some grandkids Kelis? I raised you up to be a great wife. You need a man in your life. You need to get married. I need to show you and your new husband off to my friends. It's just a phase...*' Blah- blah- blah- blah-blah. You're my home girl, my friend; I have enough detailed information on your background that could prevent *anyone* from wanting you so let's not go there please."

Before I could respond to her comment Sonia interrupted us.

"Hey ladies I made us some mimosa's to get our day started."

I looked at Keke and she was stepping out of the shower.

"Finally, someone who knows how to put a smile on my face," Keke said.

We all grabbed a glass of champagne from the serving tray Sonia was holding, lifted our glasses and made a toast.

"To healthy friendships!" Sonia said.

"To steaming hot succulent sex!" Keke said.

"To relaxation!" I added.

Keke went into her bedroom to continue getting dressed and Sonia and I worked on our makeup in her restroom.

"What do you think about Keke?" I said to Sonia.

"Keke is Keke. She's a beautiful person inside and out. I could care less about her sexual orientation. As long as she remains a loyal friend we're good."

"Oh so you overheard us talking?" I asked Sonia.

"Yes! That's why I brought the mimosas. I know she can be a little blunt at times, but that's what I love about her. It doesn't matter if the truth hurts or not, if I'm looking for the straight honest truth, she's my go to person. Ease up on her about things that she has no control over."

"But that's the thing Sonia. She does have a choice. She could do a lot better for herself."

"What do you think she's doing? She moved away on her own, has two careers that she actually loves and is passionate about. What more can a girl ask for?"

"A *man*!"

"Look I have a man, you had a man, she doesn't even want a man. That's her life. Mind your business. You're starting to overstep boundaries now. I mean if you have a problem with it, why are you friends with a person who's a homosexual?"

"That's the thing. I was there. We were there when Keke had about three and four men at a time on lock. Men fall all over her everywhere we go. I just feel like she isn't really gay and if she is I don't want my good friend going straight to hell."
Sonia just stood there shaking her head with tears in her eyes.

"You just don't get it do you?" Sonia asked.

"Hey dolls! Are you two ready to go down for breakfast?" Keke interrupted.

"Yes we're done. I'm famished!" I stressed.

Quickly changing the subject, we headed down to the hotel restaurant for breakfast and brunch. We asked if we could sit near the open view of the hotel's lobby which had a corner view of the ocean. The lobby was overcrowded with a group of high school students who appeared to be on a senior trip because they were escorted by chaperones. One of the adults who were chaperoning the group was a stud. She was tall; brown skinned, and wore dreadlocks just past her shoulders. I had to take a double take because I thought she was a man until Keke said, "Damn, now that's the perfect eye candy over there." Sonia and I looked over.

"She is sexy Keke. Go get her girlfriend!" Sonia told her.

"She?" I asked astonished. "I thought that was a guy!"

"C'mon Syn. She's obviously a beautiful woman. This is why I must always look fabulous in public. Sexy ass chics like her give me a run for my money. Look at her muscles." Keke was obviously very attracted to her. I actually thought she was handsome too, before finding out her true gender. As we continued to stare I noticed there were two other adults, a white woman and a Pakistani man who was really sexy, helping her distribute the room keys to the students.

"It seems like there are options for you as well Syn." Keke said laughing.

"Girlfriend I am not interested in men who have a different nationality than me." I responded. "Unless it's an older wealthy white man, and that only occurs occasionally."

"You could be missing out on your blessings limiting yourself to *black* men and old wealthy white men. You have a history of losers; pick a winner for a change." Keke said sarcastically.

I thought back to that feeling of neglect I experienced when I dealt with Drake's five years of bullshit.

"I never thought I'd be saying this, but you two are right! I deserve better than I've gotten. I can't believe I thought turning to older men was the answer." I said.

"It's okay to make a few mistakes here and there," Keke said.

"We all deserve better." Sonia mumbled under her breath.

Keke and I looked over at her.

"What do you mean by "we" Sonia? You're about to get married next month and you and

Terrence have made it through probably one of the largest storms a relationship could have possibly endured." Keke said.

"Yeah, I agree." I looked over at Sonia. "What's the problem?" I asked out of curiosity. Tears began running down her face and she put her head down.

"It's just so disheartening and challenging that's all. From his health, to our financial issues, to the two miscarriages I've had, to evidence of him cheating, and he..." Sonia paused for a second.

"He what Sonia?" Keke asked.

"He beats me." Sonia revealed.

"He beats you!?!" Keke shouted.

"Shhh let's keep our voices down. We don't want to cause a ruckus down here." I told them.

"Our girl just exposed her dude and all you can say is, *"Let's keep our voices down?"* See you and I used to bump heads and you're starting to piss me the hell off right now and our vacation has hardly even begun."

"I don't mean it like that Keke," I said.

"Damn have some compassion for her. You act like you're on Terrence's side or know something she doesn't know!" Keke yelled out.

"Wait, calm down ladies! I've been dealing with this for some time now. I think I'm just emotional about everything because I have a sense of freedom and I'm actually considering calling the whole thing off." Sonia interjected.

"Baby girl, you have to do what's best for you and Jaxon." Keke stressed. "Has he seen his dad put hands on you?"
I sat there and listened while Sonia wiped her tears before attempting to respond to Keke.

"Jax hadn't seen him physically abuse me until a few weeks ago."

"That's not good Sonia." Keke told her.

"Trust me love, I'm aware of that. He's also had other women around him."

"And how do you figure that?" I asked.

"Jax has mentioned it before. One day after work on our ride home from daycare he says to me, 'Mommy. I want you to meet Jayla, Jaden, and Ms. Journey.' And I asked him who they were and he responded, 'Jayla and Jayden are twins and Ms. Journey is their mom. She gives us candy whenever they come around and she and Daddy tell us to go play on the playground while they play in the car.' Sonia said crying.

"Oh wow! So of course you asked Terrence about it right?" Keke asked.

"I tried asking him, but every time I attempt to address something I don't like, he becomes verbally and physically abusive so I just try avoiding it." Sonia said.

"When did all this start?" I asked out of curiosity. "Every time I come over, you all appear to be so happy."

"That's the thing Syn; we *appear* to be happy. I'd have to say it started a little while after he was diagnosed with prostate cancer. Terrence and I use to be the best of friends and talk about everything from our past, dreams we mutually shared for our son and our future kids, our goals, and being together forever. And somewhere along the way he just lost interest in me. We haven't had sex in six months. I tried wearing lingerie the night before flying here and he just pushed me away. I haven't even spoken to him. I texted to let him know we made it safely and he hasn't even responded."

"Everything will be okay Sonia. You just need some time to think logically. Either you two get the help that you need to be better life partners or you get ghost." Keke advised her.

"Get ghost? What's that Keke?" She asked lost.

"It means to pack up your shit and your son and get the hell out of that loft," Keke informed her. "I know you all are living large and things, but you make enough money to maintain your lifestyle without his trifling ass. Do you know the psychological damage that can be done to that baby?"

"I know Keke. I have a lot to consider." Sonia said sighing.

"Yes you do." I added.

We finished our drinks and paid our tab before heading out to the beach. Coincidently, the students and their chaperones had setup on the beach as well.

"You all go ahead. I need to make a phone call I'll catch up with you shortly." I told them. I went back upstairs to use my cell phone in private.

"Hello." Terrence spoke.

"You bastard!" I yelled.

"What are you talking about now Syn?"

"You didn't tell me you were seeing another woman. And not to mention you've been putting your hands on Sonia? What the fuck is your problem?" I screamed through the phone's receiver.

"Listen bitch!" He said.

"Bitch? Who the hell do you think you're talking to? I will ruin your life you little dick fucker."

"Savannah you mean absolutely nothing to me but a piece of ass, so for you to question my whereabouts and my personal business that doesn't concern you is out of line. You just make sure you say what you have to say and get the footage I need so that we can get this money."

"You know, I'm starting to doubt this whole plan. Sonia doesn't need or deserve a piece of shit ass punk like you and neither do I!"

"Ha!" he said laughing. "That shit sounds crazy coming out of the same mouth you sucked my dick with. You're the same slut who begged me to come over to bless with some going away stroking. Like I said before, if you want my homeboy Drake back, you'll play the cards I've dealt for you. Now I will talk to you when you return home." Terrence said sarcastically.

"Well what about..." Terrence had disconnected the line before I could speak. Ugh he just makes my blood boil! I should get back downstairs before they suspect something.

Keke and Sonia had ordered us drinks and their glasses were half empty.

"Well it took you long enough! Where have you been?" Keke asked. "We're almost done with our second round."

"I went back to the room to call my bank," I lied. "And I stopped by the gift shop to purchase this hat I'm wearing." I added.

"Oh cute!" Sonia said.

"Thank you! Well I'm happy to see that you're in a better mood Sonia."

"You know I can't stand to be around negative energy for too long so I changed that quick!" Keke said proudly.

"Good! Oh and I see you ladies aren't too far from your eye candy." I noticed the two ladies and the gentleman from the lobby were only about 10ft away from us. The guy wasn't wearing a shirt and his body was tight and muscular. I started to rethink my decision of choosing to limit myself to black and white men. He began rubbing sun tanning lotion on the Caucasian woman. The more I watched the more observant I became and happened to notice wedding bands on both of their hands.

"Oh they're married!" I told the girls. Keke looked over and said, "No they're not. She doesn't even look like someone he would even date." The lady was pale, thin, and frail. He was the total opposite: tanned, healthy, and strong.

"Well you never know guys. Opposites attract quite often. And if they work together it's much easier to meet someone you have plenty in common with." Sonia reminded us.

"Yeah you're right. Let me stop pre-judging. We haven't even formally introduced ourselves. There's only one way to find out." Keke said before going over to their area.

"I can't believe she just walked right over." I said shocked.

"C'mon Syn you know Keke. She doesn't mind meeting and talking to new people. Nothing frightens her." Sonia stated.

The three of them looked over while Keke stood there shaking their hands one at a time. Soon after talking with them briefly, Keke and the stud walked over to us.

"Girls meet Lex. She's a basketball coach. These are my girls from college Sonia and Syn. We reached out our hands and she gave us each a firm handshake.

"Greetings ladies. It's very nice to meet you." Lex said as she shook our hands.

"Wow you have a heavy accent. Are you Jamaican?" I asked her.

"Yes mi ladi, I am Jamaican." Lex replied.

"So do you coach the girls or boys basketball team?" Keke asked her.

"A likkle bit of both." Lex explained.

"Interesting..." Keke said while admiring her muscles from behind.

"Well it was nice meeting you as well Lex. Take care." Sonia told her.
She smiled and walked away.

"That's one sexy chocolate thang there." Keke said while biting her bottom lip.

"Girl did you get the digits?" Sonia asked.

"Wait! Before answering her, are the other two married or not?" I asked.

"Yes they're married. But not to each other." Keke revealed.

"But they were just over there kissing." Sonia stated.

"Um yeah. It's complicated." Keke said shaking her head smiling.

"Relationships just aren't relationships anymore." Sonia said sadly.

"Who are you telling?" I said agreeing. We ordered another round of drinks and double shots of Tequila. Then we people watched for a while and tanned before heading back upstairs to reminisce and catch up once we were done with our drinks.

Chapter 5

Girl Talk

After unlocking our door I stumbled in almost knocking over one of the floor lamps. Keke tripped over her flip-flops while Sonia ran to the bathroom to vomit. It was pretty obvious that we were one wasted crew of ladies. I lit a few candles, opened the French doors to let a breeze come in and poured us a bottle of Sweet Red wine. We gathered some pillows from the couch and made a pallet on the floor.

"Okay, who's going first?" Keke asked excitedly.

"First with what?" I asked.

"Who's going first with their most erotic sexual experiences?" Keke explained.

"Duh Syn!" Sonia yelled. "You know Keke's the biggest freak of us all. Something about sex was soon to come."

"Well you go first Keke!" I said loudly.

"No I'd rather be bored with one of your stories instead." Keke said to us sarcastically.

"Okay. I'll go first and trust me you won't be bored." Sonia stressed confidently. "And this stays between these walls might I add."

We all raised our right hand and pinky promised each other while reciting aloud, "*I promise to refrain from deliberately mentioning my sister's business to any other individual outside of our circle. I promise to always keep it within my own mind and these four walls.*" Without notice she began talking.

"It was a cold, rainy and windy winter night. I was traveling home from a late meeting when suddenly my car spun out of control. Luckily no one was traveling in front or behind me. I was fine, but my front passenger tire had blown out. I immediately called Terrence, but he never picked up. So instead of continuing to wait alone in the dark, I called roadside assistance and this tall gentleman arrived maybe 15 minutes at most dressed in a tan buttoned down uniform shirt and navy blue slacks. He was like my knight in shining armor. Needless to say he ended up helping me in more ways than one."

"I knew your ass had a little hoe-dom in you somewhere." Keke said jokingly.

I smacked my lips. "Keke let her finish! And it's whoredom not hoe-dom." I told her.

"Whoredom or hoe-dom it's all the same!" Keke said.

"Continue Sonia," I said.

"So he walks over to the passenger side and knocks on the window. I rolled it down and he says with a deep voice, 'Are you okay?' Then I responded, 'I'm much better now that you're here.' He smiled at me saying, 'Glad I can save you from your troubles.' Then he winked at me! I must have wet my panties right then and there. He proceeded to change my tire and then he said, 'I don't usually do this, but you're gorgeous and if it isn't too much to ask, I'd love to take you out for a cup of coffee.' I smiled and replied, 'Aww I'm very flattered and that's awfully sweet of you, but my man wouldn't agree with that.' 'Your man huh? Well if you were my woman, you wouldn't have to call roadside assistance because I'd be assisting you with all of your daily needs.'

'Oh you're a bit cocky I see.' I said to him.

'No. I'm not cocky just confident. Listen. I'm not trying to waste your time or run any game on you. I'm only trying to see that beautiful smile of yours for an hour or two longer.'

"I began blushing and my panties got even more moist than before. God knows I had no

business even thinking about another man, but Terrence was neglecting me and I hadn't gotten a compliment from him in a while so I obliged."
Sonia paused for a moment before continuing.

"Okay, tell us more." I told her.

"Dang Syn! Let me take it all in. I'd forgotten just how fun and spontaneous that was." Sonia stated before continuing her story.

'I don't even know your name.' I said to him. "He leaned inside the passenger window so that I could read his name tag." 'Jeffrey is it?' I asked him.

'Yes, but call me Jeff.'

'Okay Mr. Jeff, when were you thinking of having coffee with me?' I asked.

'How does right now sound?'

'Right now?' I chuckled. 'What about the company's truck? Aren't you on the clock?' I asked.

'Yes, but I'm on my own clock. It's my company. Roadside assistance calls local companies closest to their client who is in need of assistance.' Jeff stated.

'Oh. So kind of like a third party?'

'Exactly! So just follow me um...' "He reached out his hand."

'I'm sorry it's Sonia.' I revealed.

He smiled, 'So Ms. Sonia, Lydia's Coffee Shoppe is right up the road.'

'Okay, after you Jeffrey.' I said jokingly.

"Get to the nasty part!" Keke yelled.

"I'm getting there hot mama. Calm down." Sonia told Keke.

"We arrived at Lydia's Coffee Shoppe, but by then it had started pouring down raining. Suddenly my phone rings and it's him. He'd gotten my number from my insurance agency when they called him."

'Hey beautiful it's Jeff. I'll run in there and get the coffee since it's pouring out here. What would you like?'

'That's kind of you Jeffrey. I'd like an Espresso Granita double shot please.'

"Jeff ran in and purchased a cup of coffee and bottled water. He returned to his truck with my coffee in tow. Shortly after I received a text from him stating, 'How bad do you want your Espresso?' I replied, "Badly." Then he texted, 'Follow me.' So I did."

"Oh this is getting interesting!" Keke said.

"So did you follow him?" I asked.

"Of course I did. I wanted my coffee." I told them smiling. "10 minutes into our ride we pulled up to a secluded warehouse. Jeff approached my door with an umbrella and told me to get out of my car. We made it to the front entrance of the building quickly. When he opened the door of the warehouse I was intrigued by what I was seeing. There were beautiful canvas art pieces scattered throughout the entire bottom floor of the warehouse. The left side of the wall was painted white and displayed soft, beautiful, peaceful art all while the right side of the wall was painted black and displayed somewhat disturbing, evil, and dark art work. LED lights were plastered throughout displaying every piece of work aesthetically and gracefully."

'Wow! Did you paint all of this?' I asked him.

'Yes beautiful I did, and if you don't mind I'd love to paint you one day.'

'Really? I've always wanted a painting of myself. That would be awesome!' I said excitedly.

'Let's make it happen now.' Jeff suggested.

'Right this moment 'right' now?' I asked shocked.

'Sure. Why not?' He asked.

'Okay well if you insist.'

"He took my coat and handed me my coffee."

'Wait here.' He instructed.

"Jeff went upstairs to a lofted area and I sat on the ottoman that was near the front door, sipped my coffee, and waited patiently."

'Come upstairs!' He yelled down.

"Complying, I left my things by the door and headed upstairs. It was even more impressive than the downstairs area. The first thought that came to mind was that Jeff must have lived and worked there. The upstairs area was a unique living space. One side was setup like a studio which seemed to be used for photography, painting, and tattooing. The other side included a small bright yellow kitchen, an eating table for two, a Queen sized bed, black leather sectional, and double doors which lead to a balcony. Everything was neatly organized, labeled, and strategically put together perfectly. Jeff picked up a remote and music came from the speakers that were hidden behind the walls. I sat on the loveseat which was located in the studio space while he gathered his painting materials and tools."

'This place is nice. Do you live here?' I asked.

'This is my getaway spot. I lived here before I got married. Sometimes I rent it out to artists. I also do freelancing work here as well.'

'So you're married?' I asked him.

'Legally separated actually, but we still live together.'

'Interesting.' I said.

'Sonia, it isn't what you're thinking. We've been out of love for a while now. Of course I wish it could have worked, but we out grew one another over time.'

'How long were the two of you together?'

'We were married for five years, and together for seven. He said. 'But there's no need to get uncomfortable. I'm the only person who has a key to the building unless someone is renting the space and my ex is actually seeing someone else.' Jeff shared.

'Well are you dating anyone?' I questioned.

'I've dated here and there and I'm seeing someone, but it's nothing serious.' He revealed. 'What about you? What's your story?'

'Uhm I'm actually engaged. We've been together since college so about six years.' I told him.

'Are you happy?' Jeff asked. 'Well are you satisfied?'

'Things are good.' I answered.

'I knew the answer before I asked you. I can look at you and see he is no longer putting a smile on your face.'

He stated confidently.

'Wow is it that obvious?' I asked looking at him.

'Yes it is. Come on over to the couch. I think it'll be nice to paint you while you drink your coffee and stare out at the city skyline.' He suggested.

"I walked over to the couch and sat down." 'What would you like me to do now Mr. Jeffrey?' "I asked him while moving my body in a sensual manner."

'Just relax. Unbutton your top buttons and remove your suit jacket. Go into deep thought as you would after a long hard day of work.'

"I blushed as I looked over at him while slowly removing my buttons. I threw my jacket at him and it fell to the floor. He picked it up and brought it back over to me and folded it across the back of the couch. Jeff reached down and kissed me on my forehead. As he leaned up to step away, I kissed him on his lips. I felt myself wildly attracted to him. When our lips touched I knew instantly that I wanted to put it on him, but my mind kept reminding me to snap out of it. Jeffrey however, had it on his mind as well. He later shared that it had been a while since he'd been touched, kissed, or held by a woman. He grabbed my hair and gently pulled my hair tie from around my ponytail. My hair fell to my shoulders and he passionately kissed my neck while continuing to unbutton my blouse exposing the black lace bra I wore underneath. Jeff slowly suckled on my cleavage then stuck his warm strong hands under my skirt and began fondling my vagina through the black lace panties I wore. Wanting more of his gentle caress I pushed him off of me then straddled him from behind. I wanted him to feel me over- flowing so I slid my panties to the side and grabbed his hand and placed it on my clit. We both moaned excessively as we let our guards down to receive what we had both been missing. His hands touched every crevice of my body. We shared a certain kind of emptiness which allowed us to interact with each other while separating from the world. He was my escape and I was his. The feelings we shared for the two people we would have died for were mutual, but they could have cared less if we existed or not. Our situations spun our love affair in fast speed. It happened overnight drowning out my daily pain and embarrassment I often silently encountered from my heartache."

"So in other words, you two messed around on more than one occasion?" I asked.

"Something like that, Syn." Sonia answered calmly.

"Well I'm glad you got your groove on here and there Sonia because I was beginning to worry about you allowing Terrence to get his while you remained faithful to his dog ass." Keke mentioned.

"Why would you say 'with his dog ass' as if you're implying he's a dog?" Sonia asked Keke.

"Even though I live in Texas, I still get the scoop on you and Syn. And I heard he's unfaithful and that he always has been." Keke said.

"That's kind of harsh Keke." I told her.

"I'm not trying to be harsh Syn. I'm just answering Sonia's question. You know I'm the most unbiased friend you two have ever met. I don't mean any harm by it. Of course if I hear something about the two of you, whether it's true or not, I'm taking up for you." Keke explained.

"Have you heard anything bad about me or Drake?" I asked Keke.

"Yeah I heard Drake has about three kids with three different women and another on the way and neither of them are yours." she said.

"Well it's somewhat true. They're not sure if this last child is his." I told her.

"Can't we just change the subject of this he say she say shenanigans?" Sonia suggested.

"I agree." Keke said. "As a matter of fact, I'll start with one of my juicy love scenes."

"Wait, bathroom break!" I yelled out.

"It's time for more refills too!" Sonia yelled.

"Okey dokey. I'll just sit here and wait for you chicas to return." Keke told us. Soon we were back in the living room lounging on the floor pallet we created earlier. Keke got two more pillows from the sofa and leaned on them while she faced the two of us. Then immediately she began telling her story.

"It had been a while since I'd last been caressed by her, since she'd started dating an older woman who'd completely grasped most of her time and attention. I invited her over for a bite to eat and cooked her favorite: barbecue chicken, baked beans, potato salad, and cornbread. 'Maybe after she eats dinner we can devour each other,' is what I thought just before she came over to my flat. I showered after being on the road for the last 7 hours."

"Where'd you go?" Sonia asked interrupting.

"I'd gone to New Orleans for a mandatory conference." Keke shared.

"Are you sure it wasn't a mandatory dominatrix session?" I asked laughing.

"Hell no girlfriend! I saved it all for her. That sexy caramel thang still has my kitty kat whimpering." Keke said laughing. "Anyway, refreshed and excited to see her, I decided at the last second that I would make banana pudding, which is her favorite dessert."

"You were doing it big for her I see." I said sarcastically. Keke laughed before continuing.

"About an hour or so later, she arrived at my place with a bottle of wine and that smile that could brighten up a funeral. I'd pre-rolled a blunt so that she wouldn't need to. Even though smoking and sexual acts were our forte' for me, it was much deeper than that. She had my heart soon after she introduced herself to me. Moody had always been polite, genuine, sweet, and kind, but it was her thug-like characteristics which kept my kitty super moist and myself (chuckles) well let's just say; very engaged."

"Hmm sounds like she was a beast." Sonia stated. Keke smiled and quickly had a moment to reminisce just before continuing.

"Yes, yes; she's a beast to say the least."

"What kind of name is 'Moody'?" I asked out of curiosity.

"The kind of name you give a person who has different mood swings. Duh Syn!" She flipped her hair then continued. "We sat on the couch and talked while we smoked. Afterwards we ate our food and decided to go into the bedroom for a nightcap."

"Oooh bring on the exciting part!" Sonia yelled excitedly.

"I'm trying!" We all laughed. "She followed behind me and I held on to her hand while pulling her into the bedroom. I shoved her onto my bed before climbing on top of her. I kissed the side of her neck since it's the spot that gets her instantly hot. Moody sat up and flipped me over. She started kissing me very gently and passionately. Moving down my body slowly, she lifted up my top and started to bite my nipples. I gripped her head firmly while pulling on her dreads. I forced myself back on top, flipping her unexpectedly.

'Scratch my back Moody.' She moaned and did as I told her. 'Now pull my hair, sexy.' Gripping my hair with one hand, she pulled me closer into her pelvis. Straddling her I began riding her as if she was already strapped. I wanted to feel her so badly. I was ready for both pain and pleasure.

'Go strap up, sexy.' I told her before hopping off of her. She went into the bathroom carrying her black bag along with her. As I sat impatiently, I decided to strip the comforter from the bed and replace the white lightbulbs with blue lightbulbs. I pulled a whip, handcuffs, and anal beads from my lamp table. The colored lighting was just enough light to see one another. She came out of the bathroom in a black tee and boxers. The print coming from her boxers revealed there was more than just her body to look forward to. I wanted her right then and there. I jumped up and met her in the doorway. Wearing only a black thong and a lustful grin, I wrapped my arms around her neck and hugged her tightly. Immediately after ripping her shirt off I kissed every part of her chest. I removed her underwear piece by piece just before leading her back to my bed. I turned towards the bed and started crawling with my back facing her. Before getting comfortable she took me from behind by my throat and unveiled her strap... My mouth watered instantly. She ripped my thong to pieces and placed her dick at the entrance of my anal. Suddenly cum ran down my thigh onto my leg. She whispered in my ear, 'Taste me.' With no hesitation I turned around, grabbed her dick with my mouth without using either of my hands, slurped it, and put it in my mouth. She moaned and scratched my back while I pleasured her. Moody whispered my name, 'Keke. You're so good at what you do baby.' "Lifting my head just enough to speak briefly I replied, 'I know I am,' and I went back to enjoying her dick in its entirety."

"My God this is so damn gay!" I shouted covering my ears.

"Syn if you don't hush your disrespectful partially Christian ass up." Keke told me.

"Okay okay, I'll be quiet, but don't get too explicit for my virgin ears. You know I can't stand to hear about same sex hook ups. It just makes me extremely uncomfortable."

"Hell I don't know why, you fucked all five starters of Morehouse college basketball team!" Keke shouted sarcastically. She looked at Sonia. "Now that my sistah, should make a bitch uncomfortable."

"Whatever, Keke! God never said it was okay to sleep with the same sex." I told her.

"God never said its okay to sleep with lots and lots and lots and a lot more lots of the opposite sex either." Keke said rolling her eyes.

"Well ladies it's okay...Let's not get into a little spat of past and current decisions we or shall I say, the two of you have chosen to get into for your very own purposes. I don't know about you two, but I'm kind of tired. Can I borrow one of your phones please?" Sonia asked. "Mine died while we were sitting out on the beach."

"My phone is somewhere dead too!" Keke told Sonia. "Use Ms. High and Mighty's phone. It seems to be the only one with a full charge." I quickly placed my phone underneath my right thigh realizing I'd programmed Terrence's name as Big Daddy in my contacts. Sonia reached her hand out for me to pass her my phone.

"C'mon Syn. Let me borrow your phone real fast." Sonia said.

"I'm playing Candy Crush on my phone. Just call him from the landline. We don't mind paying for the extra expenses."

"Uh speak for yourself, Syn!" Keke shouted while smacking her lips and rolling her eyes. "Just give her your phone real quick so that she can check in with her boo before bed, heffa."

"Well I'd rather pay those charges than what it will cost to dial back home from my cell." I said; hoping that would work.

"Be selfish with your things then, Syn! Good night Ladies! I'm exhausted." Sonia stated before heading to her selected bedroom.

Keke turned around and looked at me before speaking. "Hoe you could have let her use your phone. You can be so rude and stingy at times."

"I'd rather be a hoe than a dyke any day of the week." I told Keke while walking away from her intended sarcasm.

"Wait what did you just call me?" Keke asked as she got up from the floor to follow me. "I didn't hear you clearly." I turned around and spoke slowly, "I- said- I'd- rather- be- a- hoe -instead –of- a –dyk..." Keke slapped me directly in my mouth before I could finish repeating what I'd originally told her. I held my jaw for a brief moment then shoved her back down to the floor. We tussled for a split second before Sonia ran back in to break us up.

"Oh my God ladies! What the hell?" Sonia yelled once we were apart. "Listen I have to fight and put up with senseless acts of violence in my home. I came on vacation to get away from drama and now you two have brought it within our little retreat. No No No! This cannot and will not continue. I set out to have a good ol' time with my girls. Save this petty non-sense for another time!" Sonia walked off angrily slamming her bedroom door behind her.

"She's right you know." I told Keke.

"Yeah on so many levels she is." Keke said agreeing. "Listen. I apologize for slapping you, but I have a temper and you have a mouth on you that could piss off a priest. Let's just agree to disagree." She reached her hand out to me.

"I will watch my mouth if you agree to control your temper and how you react to everything that I say to you." I told her.

"That's fair. Good night."

"Good night Keke." She turned off the music and I put the pillows back on the couches where they belonged. We turned the lights off and headed our separate ways.

CHAPTER 6

Play Time

The next morning, Keke prepared for her early morning appointment. She had gone to the gym and back in time to make us breakfast even before Sonia and I were up for the day. She'd left a note next to our plates she had prepared and wrapped in saran wrap. The note read, *Good morning Divas! I wanted to apologize again for last night. Enjoy breakfast and have a morning spa session on me. I will speak to you ladies after I've taken special care of my new clients. Ciao until later!*

"Well that was nice of her!" Sonia mentioned.

"Yes it was a great gesture." We ate our breakfast, got dressed and headed for the hotel spa. When we walked up to the door, we didn't even have to open it. We we're immediately being catered to by these two handsome island guys. Sonia and I searched through the spa options, but the guys insisted that we follow them because our dear friend Keke had arranged for the Ladies Night spa package which consisted of the guys giving us a full body massage, facials, fruit and wine in between sessions, a foot rub, and a mud bath. So much stress and tension was being released as we continued to enjoy each part of the services rendered.

"I wonder what our girl is up to." Sonia said.

"Who knows? She's probably hanging from chandeliers or something." I joked. We laughed and closed our eyes as we went back to enjoying our one on one spa time.

Keke knocked on the door of Rachel and Tony's penthouse suite around 10:15 am. Rachel answered the door with a cup of green tea in her hand. She was wearing a long navy blue satin night gown. Her hair was pulled up and styled in pin curls and her French pedicure was slightly hidden by the length of her gown.

"Good morning Keke! Welcome!" Rachel told her.

"Good morning Rachel! Are you two just about ready to get started?"

"Well sure. Tony will be out of the shower soon. We kind of had a morning session of our own if you know what I mean." Rachel said smiling.

"Judging by the elevator incident, I'm sure you two had an amazing time. So while he's in the shower I'd like for you to review this document and sign and date it at the bottom. It's just a non-disclosure agreement."

"Sure I can take care of that while he's finishing up. It will give us one less thing to do." Rachel signed the document without reading it.

"Okay so since that's taken care of, take off your gown." Keke instructed Rachel. Slightly reluctant, Rachel took her orders well. "Now hop on your fitness ball." She walked over to the area designated for their mini gym equipment. "Lie back on the ball." Rachel's nipples became erect soon after placing her back on the cool rubber fitness ball. "Now relax. Breathe in and breathe out slowly. I want you to listen to your heartbeat and the sounds of the ocean. Pretend that I'm not even here." Rachel took deep breaths. "I'm going to touch you now." Keke grabbed baby oil from her bag and placed her right hand on Rachel's inner thigh and her left hand on her abs. "Continue to breathe Rachel." Keke directed. Rachel's breaths soon turned into moans. "Keep breathing Rachel."

"But it feels so good!" She said groaning.

"I'm certain that it does, but I need you to concentrate on the ocean." Keke reminded her. Tony walked out of the shower with a white towel wrapped around the lower half of his body. He was mighty ripped for an older guy.

"Hello Keke. I see you two have gotten started without me."

"Hi Tony. Actually you're right on time. Come on over." Keke said inviting Tony to join them.
"I need you to kneel down right in front of your woman." Tony obeyed and walked over towards Rachel and kneeled down in front of the fitness ball.

"Okay. Now, what would you like me to do?" He asked.

"Close your eyes and relax. I want you to inhale and exhale nice and slowly. Once you've gotten your breathing under control, I need you to focus on the sounds of the ocean." Tony closed his eyes and caught onto the breathing exercise quickly. Rachel opened her eyes to peak at her man.

"Shut your eyes Rachel!" Keke yelled before tapping Rachel's breasts with her leather fun paddle.

"Oooohhh!" Rachel screamed. Tony opened his eyes losing his concentration as well.

"What am I missing ladies?" Tony asked interested.

"There isn't anything going on that you wouldn't approve of Poppa." Rachel answered.

"Relax!" Keke stressed once again. "I guess I need to quickly take charge of this exercise before it gets completely out of hand." Keke ripped the bath towel from Tony's waist revealing his naked body. Startled by her actions, Tony's heart began to race rapidly. Keke pushed him to the floor and went over to Rachel and pulled her by her hair forcing her to sit down on Tony's face. Without Keke's permission, Tony satisfied Rachel until she reached an orgasm. While Tony fed off of Rachel's vagina, Keke strapped herself with one of the newest strap-ons just recently advertised as *the best lamb skin* ever invented.

"Oh Poppa that was the best head I've ever had!" Rachel said flabbergasted.

"I'm about to give you the best dick you've ever had." Keke said smiling. She sat on the fancy beige chaise near the doors of the balcony with her legs wide opened and the lamb skin dildo standing in a vertical position. She'd removed all of her clothes as well. Her rock hard body glistened perfectly in the sun. Rachel looked over at Keke excited to give it a try.

"Come over here and suck on it." Keke said authoritatively. Rachel didn't even take a moment to consult with Tony before crawling over to Keke on her behalf. Tony anxiously sat there in awe and observed as his lady teased Keke by licking and suckling on her nipples and down her crotch only to deep throat the artificial penis she was wearing.

"Like this?" Rachel asked Keke.

"Yes beautiful! Now spit on it." Keke motioned Rachel's head up and down with her hands supporting her neck as she pleasured her. Tony got off just from watching. Rachel's moans created a rhythmic tone as Keke and Tony began to admire Rachel's dick sucking abilities. Rachel's hands were covered in saliva which dripped from her mouth onto the penis. "Hop on it Rachel." Keke told her as she pulled her head up and away from her strap.

"You want me to ride you?" Rachel asked stunned.

"Yes. Hop on top." Keke ordered.

"But I've never been on top before." Keke looked over at Tony. "Is she being serious?"

"Yeah. She's never been on top with me." Tony said confirming.

"That doesn't mean I can't be taught today. What do you want me to do?" Rachel asked Keke eagerly.

"Get on top. I'll assist you." Rachel felt kind of intimidated, but insisted on giving it a try.

"Shouldn't we use some lube?" Rachel asked.

"Look at it. It's already lubricated. Now go ahead and sit on it." Rachel took a deep breath and eased her labia majora around the saliva drenched penis and slid all the way down with no problem. "That's it; now squat on it then tiptoe." Keke told her. Rachel listened while Keke gripped her waist and guided her up and down the lamb skin penis. Tony's distant moans turned into groans when Rachel began screaming out Keke's name. It was obvious that Rachel was enjoying the ride, and probably a bit more than Tony actually approved of. Tony was a wealthy, anything goes type of guy, but when it came down to his black queen Rachel, he could be somewhat overly possessive. Shortly after Rachel came on Keke, Tony walked over to the two ladies and massaged his penis just before busting all over Keke's breasts. Keke didn't really seem to mind much being that she was in character. Tony attempted to titty fuck Keke but before long he was completely soft. He then pulled Rachel off of her and made her kneel down in front of him in the doggy-style position. His penis became erect again. Just before entering her, Keke stopped him and teased him just a little. She spat in her hand and grabbed his dick. While rubbing it gracefully she smacked Rachel on her ass and entered her from behind with her fingers. Rachel seemed to enjoy being pleasured while her man's penis was in the hands of another woman. She began grinding her body back on Keke and clenched her vagina muscles right before exploding all over the carpeted floor.

"Oh God is that how that shit feels?" Rachel screamed as she continued to grind faster on Keke's fingers while she squirted. It was her first time experiencing it. Tony was so aroused by Rachel's reaction he covered her back with his cum. Keke had exceeded their expectations after a few more tricks and things she thrilled them with so they tipped her very well and invited her to their private party that was to be held later that evening. She collected her money and three personal invitations for herself, Sonia, and I.

CHAPTER 7

Mermaid

Sonia and I decided to hop back into bed after coming back from the spa and doing a slight shopping spree while we waited for Keke to return from the S/M appointment she'd set up yesterday with a couple she "supposedly" met in the fitness center. I'm not so sure how she promotes her domineering skills, but I can say the girl is a true hustler. I may not agree with her dating women, because of my religion, but money keeps me interested which is why I prefer dating older men.

When Keke returned from her session, with the married couple, she told us that we were personally invited to their private party later in the evening.

"What are we supposed to wear to this shindig Keke?" I asked.

"I was told to wear my beautiful smile," she replied glowing.

Sonia and I just stood there looking at her in amazement as she counted the 2K she'd just made within an hour.

"Dang girl! That's a lot of cash! What did you have to do for it?" I asked.

"Well, you know the basics; tied them up, gagged and spanked the husband, strapped the wife, scratched up their backs, bit their nipples, and massaged their private areas with baby oil."

"Private areas, Keke?" Girl you are acting as if we're in a professional Sex 101 class or something. Don't get bougie." We all laughed and proceeded to search for outfits.

"They did inform me that we are having dinner and dessert on the beach. I'm wearing a tight fitting black dress and heels if that helps any." Keke mentioned.

"Yes that helps a lot!" I said.

Keke added, "But be ready in approximately five hours. We need to get there on time because Rachel and Tony are anal about being on time. They specifically stated that if any guests are more than five minutes late, they wouldn't be allowed to board the yacht which will take us to their private island."

A few cocktails and outfit changes later, we all looked ravishing in our cocktail dresses. I wore a long flowing red backless dress with a diamond necklace I'd gotten on my 21st birthday from my favorite Sugar Daddy Harry. My wavy jet black hair hung down my back partially camouflaging my bare skin. Sonia looked lovely in her all white knee length A- lined lace dress. Her hair was in a bun highlighting her beautiful cheekbones. Keke looked stunning and mysterious with her black mermaid dress hugging her hips and ass for dear life, which she tried toning down by wearing a Mother of Pearl layered necklace which draped down her back with a matching clutch.

Approximately a half an hour before our expected departure time, we walked up to their yacht which read, "Fantasy Connection." There was a tall broad shouldered gentleman who greeted us. Before we were allowed to step over the threshold, Keke had to provide a password that Rachel had given her for all-inclusive privileges.

"Hi, I'm Keke party of three and I have a fantasy connection."

The young guy spoke into his headset before addressing her.

"What's the connection to your fantasy?" he asked Keke.

"*Mermaid.*" She replied whispering. He smiled and let us through the chained entrance.

"Right this way; to your left ladies." He directed.

The three of us walked behind a door that was draped with black curtains. There was a bar to the right filled with every kind of liquor and wine one couldn't have possibly had in a lifetime as well as fruity beverages we hadn't tried before. Guests were dressed in their black tie wear while female servers wore nothing but diamonds around their necks along with black string bikini bottoms leaving other parts of their bodies exposed. Rachel and Tony offered two signature drinks, one they referred to as *purple pleasures* and the other as *blue balls*. After looking around at the majority of the drinks in the other guest's glasses, it seemed as if *"purple pleasures"* was the drink of choice for most of us. Live entertainment kept us occupied as we watched in astonishment while an artist painted a naked couple right before our eyes. Lights lit up the stage while we, the onlookers, were disguised in the darkness, but our purple drinks glowed in the dark. Jazz tunes played throughout the yacht. Just as the artist finished his masterpiece of the couple in 3D, we were docking. Everyone was escorted off the yacht one by one. The people who joined us looked just as nice as we did; a crowd full of diverse, attractive, professionals looking to have a great time.

A trail of candles and white rose petals lead us to their villa. Everyone looked on as fireworks went off above our heads as we slowly traveled up the trail way.

The outside of their villa was well lit with white night lights, while flickering candles lit up the interior of the home. Once the path ended we were all given numbers and directed by servers who wore tuxedos, to go through the side door of a gate which lead to the back of the villa.

The girls and I were in awe. It was as if it were out of a movie or a backyard oasis magazine. Their back yard was the ocean. Everything was set up so beautifully. The scenery was eccentric yet very romantic and inviting. We couldn't believe our eyes.

"And this, ladies is what you call a private dinner." Keke stated.

"Wow! It's so beautiful!" Sonia said.

"It truly is! I can't believe they own all of this!" I yelled.

"Okay chicas, let's not act as if we've never seen anything as beautiful as this before." Keke told us.

"Hell we haven't!" I told Keke. There were white votive candles lining the edge of the ocean, white floating candles in the ocean, and round tables with white table cloths dressed with long stem candles and bright white centerpieces were placed so beautifully in a tent draped with white curtains. Pillars surrounded all four corners of the tent, but there wasn't anything placed on them. It was classy and elegant. We all sat at our designated table and we were soon joined by a white couple and a single black guy. Servers, male and female, satisfied our appetites with the options of fresh stuffed shrimp, filet mignon, and salmon topped with a special sauce and vegetables. We were offered the finest champagne and sparkling water. The women sipped on Armand de Brignac "Ace of Spades" Rose while the men drank "Ace of Spades" Gold. Dessert consisted of dessert pancakes with custard and berries and vanilla bean ice cream topped with chunks of pralines dressed in chocolate or caramel.

"Good evening everyone and thanks for joining us at our home for our third annual Sex Fantasy Connection." Rachel announced as she held hands with her hubby Tony. Both Sonia and I looked over at Keke.

"What?" I said whispering to Keke.

"What is she referring to Keke?" Sonia asked.

"Shhhh! Chill out you two! You are not required to do anything you don't want to do. Although if you don't participate in any of the sexual activities, you are required to walk around in the nude and clean up after everyone who is mature enough to get it in." Keke explained to us jokingly. Rachel continued speaking at a distance.

"We will start off with a few icebreakers right after dessert." Rachel stated before sitting down.

"What? Why didn't you share this with us prior to coming?" Sonia asked. I thought to myself. 'This is the perfect time to get the evidence Terrence asked for.'

"Sonia it could be fun." I added.

"Are you going to partake in any of the festivities, Syn?" Sonia asked.

I shrugged my shoulders. "I mean we're all adults and we don't know these people personally and they don't know us." I responded. The white couple who were sitting next to us excused themselves from the table.

"I guess you're right." Sonia said unsure. The black guy brought his head closer to us.

"If it helps any, this is my third year attending this event and I've never participated in a one on one session, but I have been invited to watch by several couples in one night. Rachel and Tony are laid back folks and they're very genuine kind people. Even though the rules are set in place, they don't really enforce them. But they do enforce safety and making sure everyone is comfortable with whatever they choose to do; whether that's opting in or out of the festivities."

"Thank you for clarifying that Mr..." Keke said holding her hand out to the older gentleman.

"It's D. Clark. However, you lovely ladies can call me whatever you like." He said smiling at the three of us while shaking each of our hands one at a time as we introduced ourselves.

"What if no one invites us to watch?" I asked. "Then what happens?"

"Then you choose to get on the yacht that's heading back to the hotels after dinner, clean up in the nude as Keke stated, and watch porn with a group of others who didn't make the cut, or masturbate in a dark room alone. However, if you choose to masturbate there are live cameras in the designated masturbation rooms and you will appear on camera throughout the rest of the home."

Mr. D. Clark informed us. "Oh and last, but not least, the man of the house chooses one to three ladies, he then ties them up and gags them, then takes turns having sex with each of them in a room of about 6-12 voyeurs. The on lookers are then asked to rate which girl Tony has the best chemistry with throughout the sexual acts."

"Oh? So do the participants benefit from allowing Tony to have his way with them?" Keke asked Mr. D. Clark.

"Of course they do! They are all given really nice prizes. But the prizes aren't revealed until the ratings have been announced." He explained.

"What kinds of prizes were given the last few years?" I asked him.

"Let's see." Mr. D. Clark said as he pondered. "One girl won a Porsche, another girl won a year's worth of human hair bundles, $500 cash prizes, a two week all-expense paid vacation to wherever she wanted to go in the world for two. I can say, they are professional and very selective with whom they invite to these events. Tony is a diplomat and cannot be caught up in anything that can be a hindrance to him or his family." He informed us.

"That's so interesting, yet they seem so down to earth and laid back." Sonia stated.

"Right! It's almost as if they're just as normal as you and I. But hey, like I say to you two all of the time; we are all human and can mess up from time to time. No judgment over here." Keke said looking over at me.

"What?" I asked.

"Syn c'mon now, you are the all-time favorite *Miss Goody Two Shoes*. No one can do any harm in your eyes without you feeling like Satan birthed them himself." She replied.

"I am not a Miss Goody Two Shoe... Thank you!"

"Whatever, Syn! I hope that you can prove that to us tonight." Keke said.

"I'll show you just that tonight! Just watch!" I told them confidently. Little did I know, the dark path I followed would lead to self-destruction.

CHAPTER 8

Against All Odds

"Screw this fancy stuff! Excuse me, Sir." I said to one of the servers before asking him for another round of purple pleasures for the three of us as we sat and waited for our numbers to be called. So far it seemed that everyone was participating in the sex fantasy connection. I couldn't back out now even if I wanted to. I had to prove to them that I too could fit in. I secretly wanted to be chosen by Tony. All of the prizes sounded as if acting out his sexual desires were worth it. And before I knew it, my number was called by Rachel.

"0087!" she shouted. I took back the remainder of my drink and slowly stood up from my seat.

"Oh God, is it you?" Sonia asked.

"Yes." I told her then headed to where Rachel and the others were standing.

"Ladies, you are very special. You all have been selected first which means you get to pull your destiny from this fishbowl we have filled with written fantasies and desires from some of our past participants." Rachel announced on the microphone she held in her hand. I heard Keke and Sonia rooting for me at a distance.

"Quiet down everyone! Of course we can't move along without an icebreaker." Rachel suggested. The servers passed all of the male participants a banana and asked all of the ladies to pretend we were giving fallatio to the gentlemen of our choice without the use of our hands. I walked over to this older Caucasian guy who appeared to have just as much money as Rachel and Tony because he was the only one wearing a Rolex.

'Hmmmm just the way I like them; wealthy!' I said under my breath.

Surprisingly, it was so much fun and extremely hilarious attempting to suck and eat the bananas without using our hands all while trying to squat like ladies in our cocktail dresses. Although the majority of us were trying to look sexy and be cute, there was this one lady who didn't mind putting her knees in the sand. She sucked on that black guy's banana like it was the last dick of time. When we were done, she had built up so much saliva around her mouth, some of it had trickled down to her dress, and red lipstick and chunks of mashed banana smeared all over her face. The crowd cheered as the girl with the best performance received a plastic "Super Head" trophy which was issued to the lady with the banana face, and afterwards we were able to pull fantasies from the fishbowl. There were a total of 8 of us who were able to pull. There were four males and four females. Rachel brought the fishbowl in my direction and I closed my eyes and stuck my arm in praying that I would get to have a chance to be next to Tony or the gentlemen I'd just given make believe head to. When I pulled the piece of paper from the fishbowl it read, "Give 69 to someone of the same sex." I couldn't believe what I was seeing before my eyes.

"May I pull again please?" I asked Rachel.

"Sure you can, but whatever you select this next time, you will be required to do in order to move up to the next round." She informed me.

"What happens in the next round?" I asked out of curiosity.

"The next round is when my husband decides who he wants to entertain him for the evening. And that round consists of prizes you wouldn't want to chance losing over a simple task." She shared. I contemplated on choosing again.

"Aww what the hell." I said before going back into the fishbowl hoping for another chance that will actually make more sense for my sexual and financial needs. I will not embarrass myself trying to attempt to be intimate with another woman. The thought is making me want to puke up my dinner. My heart raced before opening the note.

"Go on. Open it!" Rachel told me. This note read, "*Receive oral sex from a woman while dressed in the character of your choice.*" My eyes bucked and I tried not to make it obvious to the crowd; especially my friends. I smiled and closed the note and passed it on to Rachel. Rachel opened it, read it, and passed it on into the pile of fantasy notes that had been handpicked earlier. She smiled at me. "You look nervous."

"I am. I don't even like women!" I whispered to Rachel.

"Well, don't be too afraid, Darling. Have a few more drinks, watch some porn, and make your choice before the next round of activities. It'll be okay. Trust me it's worth the challenge." Rachel reassured me. "Just go back to your seat and someone will come and show you to your designated fantasy room."

"Okay." I walked back over to the table I shared with Keke and Sonia. They were all excited and smiling when I sat down.

"I see you opening up Ms. Thang!" Keke joked.

"Yeah I'm trying." I told her.

"So which fantasy do you have to fulfill?" Sonia asked me.

"Excuse me ladies! I'm sorry to interrupt again," Mr. D. Clark stated, "but the rules are that once you have selected your fantasy it shall not be discussed with other members of your party. From here on out, everything is confidential and unless you have been a chosen voyeur, you are not allowed to know what your friend, partner, or new associate is expected to act out for the evening." Well isn't that just lovely. I'm so glad Mr. Clark shared that information because I was about to lie my behind off.

"Let's just say, it will be interesting." I said lying, almost spitting up my liquor.

"Well at least you got out of your shell for a minute to participate in the icebreaker," Sonia said.

"Yeah and you just may find you a rich ass husband while you're at it." Keke added. I laughed along and had two more of those purple pleasures drinks. Keke and Sonia went up to pull their numbers. Soon after, a gentleman dressed in an all-black tuxedo touched me on my shoulder and gave me a name tag.

"Follow me." He whispered in my ear. Looking into his eyes reminded me of someone I knew, but I couldn't recall who. I excused myself from the dinner table and followed his lead. We stepped into a room filled with costumes and disguises.

"Flip your name tag over." He told me. I did as he instructed. "What does it say?"

"It says Amber." I informed him.

"Look around the room for the drawer with the name Amber written on it." The gentleman said. There were so many drawers labeled with names that it took me about 10 minutes to locate the drawer that was specifically assigned to me. I opened it and there were three costumes I had the option of selecting. There was Amber as the School Girl, Amber as Little Red Riding Hood, and Amber as a boxer. I immediately grabbed the boxing outfit because I felt like it was appropriate for the occasion.

"Change your clothes."

"Right here?" I asked him.

"Yes, you will remove the items you wore onto the island, and then I will scan your body to make sure you aren't wearing any wires or hidden cameras. Once you've checked out ok, you will go into the next room over and shower, shave, and wash your hair."

"Excuse me! Did you say wash my hair?"

"I did." He reiterated.

"I can't get my hair wet; I spent $400.00 getting it done just before leaving the states." I told him.

"Ma'am, I apologize, but those are the rules."

"We also just showered before coming to the party. Why are we showering again?"

"You sure do complain a lot to say you're a gold-digger." The gentleman told me. I rolled my eyes at him. "If you must know, those who have a better chance of getting chosen by Tony are required to be well shaven, properly groomed, and freshly showered. It is his wife's request that all women wear her shower gel and perfume during the sessions so that he is reminded of her, which in turn prevents him from becoming curious about another fragrance one of his concubines may have worn for him during a sexual act. It's safer that way. It is to remain as strictly sex and sex only. Emotions are not to be involved."

"I understand; somewhat." I told him.

"What are you confused about?" He asked.

"For starters if I'm not sleeping with Tony right now, what does it matter?"

"In this type of environment, anything unexpected can happen. Every woman that enters through those doors has to shower and use Rachel's fragrant soap after each encounter with another individual or individuals. You are no different." He explained.

"And what the hell makes you think I'm a gold- digger?" I asked him.

"That's because Rachel personally picked you. She only chooses gold- diggers to pay some kind of homage to all of them since that's how she became the "misses." The prizes are gifts she selected for the women who are chosen by her man. She wants the money seeking participants to give, but receive more in return. She wants them to know how it will feel if they are ever chosen by a boss dude who can take care of them financially and love them unconditionally." He informed me.

"Oh wow, that's different. I can't deny the respect I've gained for her now."

"She does have that effect on people." He said persuading me to hurry up and dress in character.

After showering and putting on my itty bitty boxing boy shorts, sports bra, hooded robe, and champion belt, I applied baby oil to my abs and my thighs. My hair was still wet from washing it in the shower, but I was thrilled with how poufy and pretty it had gotten once it was washed. I put black paint under my eyes, and applied red lipstick. I looked like a completely different woman. I looked mature and exotic. It actually gave me a boost of confidence and I immediately became up for the challenge. 'The sooner you get this done, the sooner it will end,' I said to myself.

CHAPTER 9

Fantasies Connected

After getting fully dressed in the boxing costume, the gentlemen blindfolded me before escorting me into another room. I heard someone flick the lights on. I knew this because in addition to the sound of the light switch, a flash of light crept from underneath my eye cover. A woman whispered in my ear shortly after.

"Come with me," she said. Grabbing my right hand with hers, she led the way and I followed. My palms were sweating and I was somewhat nervous. 'Think about the cash prizes Syn. It will end soon.' I reminded myself. She told me to remove my robe, belt, socks and shoes so I did.

"Step inside the pool," the young lady directed. I placed my hands in a downward position to feel exactly what I was doing. When my feet touched the bottom of the pool it reminded me of a mixture of grease and water. Although it was a distinct feeling it felt fantastic. She removed my blindfold and I was standing in a small pool filled with flowers and baby oil. My opponent was a brunette white girl with an athletic build and she wore the same costume as I did; only her bottoms were thongs. She was pretty, but nothing like I imagined. She put both of her hands in the oil and began splashing it on the bottom half of my body. The men who were watching grew excited and held up signs with what they wanted to see as she began to act out their requests. The signs read, "Slam her, rub baby oil on her body, get naked, and kiss her." They wanted us to fulfill their fantasies instantaneously. Without warning she slammed me in the pool and I ended up facedown with oil and petals all over me. Holding me down with my arms behind my back she removed the tiny shorts I wore exposing my butt. The observers rooted for her to continue.

"Wait a minute!" I told her.

"Wait for what?" She asked before forcibly flipping me over with my hips in the air and my legs and thighs hanging over her shoulders. Unexpectedly, she stuck her tongue in my vagina and I shoved her away. She pulled me closer then licked my clit. I pushed her face away, but she was much stronger than me. "Just take it." She said. I tried to calm myself down before messing up my chances of moving forward. I closed my eyes and counted to ten. Before I knew it, it was over and she was being presented with the champion belt I wore briefly before everything had begun. 'That wasn't so bad.' I thought to myself. She helped me out of the pool and showed me the way back to the shower room I'd used prior to meeting her. She held her hand out before removing her clothes to shower in the stall next to me.

"I'm Sarah by the way," she shared before placing her head under the running water.

"I'm Syn." I told her as we shook hands. "I'm sorry about before. I'm not use to being with women."

"Oh it's not a problem; going down on you was a first time experience for me too." I looked at her with an expression that implied she wasn't being completely honest.

"Are you being serious?" I asked her while washing the petals and oil from my bare body.

"Yes. I've had threesomes with guys and their girlfriends, but never once had I given oral to another woman. It was always being performed on me."

"Oh. Wow."

"You seem surprised. Was I good or something?" She asked smiling.

"I mean you were okay. I was ready to get it over with." She looked down as if I'd disappointed her.

"Maybe I can change your mind about that." Sarah said as she stepped into my shower stall and pushed me under the running water. Shoving my chest against the cold tile she kneeled down and ate me from behind. It was such a surprise that I almost panicked, but then it had begun feeling just as good as when Drake would do it. "What about now?" She asked taking a break from tasting me.

"Mmmmmm." I moaned. "That feels great." She stuck her index finger in my ass and surprisingly the guy who had escorted me into the shower earlier suddenly joined us. He was a dark chocolate muscular brother with a bald head and a beard. He wore an eye patch, but it didn't seem to deter either of us from wanting what he could supply. Sarah continued eating me out while he began to unzip his pants. He seductively slid them down to his ankles.

"Come here." He said to me while holding his dick in his hand. It was huge and dark chocolate just like the rest of his body.

"Now this is a gift from God!" I told him. Without any signs of hesitation I squeezed it and shoved it in my mouth. He almost lost his balance when it hit the back of my tonsils. I let go of it and grabbed his butt cheeks coercing him to penetrate my mouth. I gagged and I became extremely aroused when his dick started to throb. It didn't matter anymore that there was a female eating my pussy because I couldn't wait to see how wonderful his huge dick would feel deep inside of me once she finished. The more he pounded my face the wetter my pussy got. Sarah didn't stop until I squirted all over her face.

"Squirt again!" She yelled before returning to her duty of clit sucking.

"Let me help you out." The guy told her. Two of his thick fingers slid into my dripping wet pussy and three strokes in position I was ejaculating again.

"Yesssss!" I screamed. "God yessss!" "Give me some more." Sarah squatted in front of me and gobbled his balls and fingered me while I continued swallowing his pre-cum.

"Put your finger back in my ass!" I told Sarah.

"I got it." He told Sarah. "Keep doing what you're doing." Sarah juggled his balls around in her mouth. "You two are sexy as hell." We removed the remainder of his clothes and he picked me up and propped me on his dick. I sat all the way on it before I began bouncing on it. Sarah stayed on her knees and allowed him to slap her face with his balls each and every time I plopped on his dick.

"I need to suck your dick again!" I screamed. He grabbed my waist and flipped my body upside down and started eating my pussy. I squirmed while striving to hook his dick with my mouth. Sarah snatched it, briefly massaged it then put it there for me. We had a rhythm going and it felt so good. She took the hair tie that was around her wrist and tied my hair in a ponytail. The guy put his finger back in my asshole and I squirted all over his face.

"Dammmnnnn! I'm having the biggest orgasm ever!" I announced. My moans and screams echoed the entire shower room and I hoped no one outside of them heard me. He kept finger fucking me while using my pussy as an adventure map. His tongue covered my sugar snatch in its totality. Everything on him was massive. He was the perfect size in the most relevant places. He put me down and I immediately fell when my feet touched the ground. "I'm too weak to stand I told them." He picked me up and carried me over to the benches that were near the lockers.

"I didn't cum yet. You wouldn't want me to leave without cumming for you right Amber?" He asked jokingly with an enticing grin on his face. Placing me in a missionary position, he jerked off before tracing my vagina Mohawk with his penis. "I thought I told you to shave everything?"

"You did." He looked at me like he was about to punish me for not following his instructions. He stuck his dick deep inside of me. "Mmmhhhmmmm." I said before he began talking smack with every stroke.

"Well (stroke), why (stroke), didn't (stroke), you (stroke), listen (stroke), to (stroke), me (stroke)?" he asked. I was so turned on I started to throw it back at him as I answered him.

"Because (stroke), I'm (stroke), a (stroke), grown (stroke), ass (stroke), woman (stroke), and (stroke), I (stroke), didn't (stroke), want (stroke), to (stroke), be (stroke), bald (stroke), like (stroke), a (stroke), darn (stroke), kid (stroke)." He moaned and just as he grew weak he stopped and told me to sit up because he wants to cum in my mouth. He signaled for Sarah to come on over and take part.

We were both anticipating his cream in and around our mouths.

"Here you go! Shit! Catch this shit!" He yelled while we kneeled with our mouths opened. "Yeahhhhh! That's right! Catch this shit!" I sucked the remaining cream from his dick and although unanticipated, he was ready for more. He pulled Sarah and put her on the bench in a doggy style position. "Come lay in front of her so that she can eat that juicebox." I went to the bench and laid on my back in front of Sarah's face. He fucked Sarah while she ate my sugar snatch some more. The view was so sexy and I never thought I would ever experience anything like it. He enjoyed pleasuring the both of us and I was beginning to get use to her devouring me. She did it so well and he's so darn handsome. He reminded me of an older gentleman named Peter whom I dated my freshmen year in undergrad. While Sarah took his dick and pleased me I began reminiscing about Peter and I and how we met. We both sat at a four seated table in the library and an hour before it closed we were the only two left inside. I looked over at him after I felt him staring at me. I was very horny at the time because I was writing an assigned research paper on S&M for a sexuality class. I kept crossing my legs and moving in my chair. He sent me a message via our school's chat line.

"Are you okay over there?" He typed.

"Who's this?" I replied.

"I'm the handsome gentlemen sitting three tables down from you." He responded.

"Oh is that so?"

"What?" he asked.

"You think you're handsome?" I asked.

"You don't think I am?" he typed.

"You're okay." I said. Truthfully, I'd seen him around campus and I was definitely attracted to him. He closed his laptop, grabbed the rest of his things and came over to my table. He pulled up a chair and sat next to me.

"Why didn't you just sit in one of the other chairs?" I asked him.

"Because I don't want anyone to see me do this."

"Do what?" I asked before he slid his hand up my skirt and rubbed my sugar snatch through my panties. I smiled and told him I was only playing and that I found him to be very attractive.

"Follow me." He got up from the table and I gathered my things and followed him upstairs. We went in the room that was reserved for students researching genealogy and locked the door behind us. He pulled my panties to the side while kissing my neck and slid his fingers across my pubic hair. I grabbed his penis through the sweat pants he wore and pulled it out. He had an erection before I could grip my entire hand around it. Enthralled in the heat of the moment, I secured his dick in my hand. I knelt down and unexpectedly engulfed it. He groaned at the impeccable head he received. Peter loved my mouth around his dick. In fact he enjoyed it so much that when we were dating he couldn't sleep without his penis in my mouth. He loved to rub my butt while I sucked him into an overnight coma. I was so attracted to him I allowed him to sleep with his penis in my mouth; now that's lust. I would wake up with a locked jaw at the start of our bedtime tactics, but then I eventually got used to it. It's hilarious now that I think about it, but his parents were millionaires and every semester he drove the hottest latest vehicles. He introduced me to money and designer things. It's one of those things that are difficult to break once you've experienced a lifestyle as such.

Someone knocked on the shower room door just as the gentleman and Sarah were about to orgasm immediately interrupting my thoughts.

"Unlock this door!" A woman demanded from the other side.

"Oh shit!" He yelled out. "That sounds like Rachel!" I ran into one of the showers and turned the water on while he and Sarah scrambled for their articles of clothing. "Hurry up before she unlocks it with her key!" He stressed to Sarah. Sarah slid in a blue tube top jumpsuit and flip-flops. We heard keys jingling and he hastily threw his clothes in an unlocked locker and ran to the last shower stall and hid. Rachel, Keke, Sonia, and another guy dressed in a tuxedo walked in.

"What the hell is going on in here and where the hell is Peter?" Rachel asked us. "He's supposed to be watching this door."

'Peter?' I thought to myself. 'I knew he looked familiar!'

"Um I haven't seen him." I said lying to cover his behind. Rachel looked puzzled, the well-dressed gentleman smiled. Keke stood there with her arms folded giving me a lot of sass while Sonia held her head down.

Rachel looked down at her cell phone and said, "Well according to this footage on my cell phone, you and Sarah have seen him." She informed me; shocking Sarah and I both. Peter, still nude, walked to the front with the rest of us just as we were attempting to add to the story we were developing on his behalf. Revealing his erect penis, Rachel picked up one of the bath towels that were folded on one of the racks and threw it at him.

"You are supposed to watch this door at all times Peter!" Rachel shouted.

"I know and I sincerely apologize for not upholding that rule. It's just that I recognized Amber, I mean Savannah Syn from college and I couldn't resist."

"And all of a sudden it seems as if you're incapable of following any of the rules." Peter looked stunned as if he was unaware of what she was implying. "No real names Peter!" He began to recollect what she was stating.

"You're right; my bad. Let me explain my side though." He pleaded.

"Ok go ahead." Rachel told him.

"She acted as if she didn't recognize me, but I thought maybe she was only role- playing." He said explaining. "And well I saw Sarah come behind her and I heard them moaning and shit so me and my ego decided to join them." My mouth fell open. I couldn't believe he'd make such of an announcement in front of everyone!

"I expected this to be confidential!" I yelled partially frustrated.

"Baby girl it is confidential. It remains between all of us." Peter pleaded.

"What she means Peter is that she wasn't aware that there were cameras in the locker room and there would have been a cold day in hell before she let another woman even look at her in a lustful way without going off on her." Keke mentioned. "She's just a bit embarrassed that her best friends were present to witness it."

"You two saw me?" I asked her.

"Yep." Keke said. I looked over in Sonia's direction.

"Sonia is she telling the truth?"

"Yes Syn, but no judgment over here. I have your back honey!" Sonia said giving me a pity hug.

"Alright! That's enough of the mushy stuff. Peter, get dressed and head back to your post. And do not touch anymore of the ladies!" She stressed to him.

"Yes ma'am." He walked toward the lockers and searched for his clothes.

"Did you two ladies shower properly?" Rachel asked. Sarah and I stared at each other hinting at our uncertainty. "Get back in the shower ladies and dress for your next act. We have a show to run!" Rachel walked out of the shower area bumping into Sarah on the way out. Keke and Sonia stood there waiting to chat while Peter and the other gentleman let us be.

Keke looked me up and down with her hand on her hip. "So how are you enjoying yourself you little slut puppy?" She asked laughing sarcastically. I turned around, ignored her and started taking another shower. "I'm only joking with you Syn, geez. Relax! We're all best friends for a reason. I only wanted to personally welcome you to the freak committee." She walked towards the back of the showers laughing loudly. Sonia went into the shower next to mine and started preparations for whatever was to come.

I cannot believe that just happened. One minute I'm squirting all over myself and the next I'm experiencing flat out embarrassment? I guess I owe Keke an apology. Sleeping with another female isn't as bad after all, but I may have to take out my handy drug I refer to as "thoughts be gone" and use it on them both if I intend on sticking with the original plan of collecting evidence for Terrence. I would hate for either of them to reveal this to anyone. That's something I don't believe I could endure. I'll wait until we're all together and I'll discreetly put drops of it in their drinks.

CHAPTER 10
After the Thrill

What a night! I held my head down in disbelief of how erratic and wild I acted on last night. I discovered so much about myself it feels surreal. The consumption of plenty of alcohol, weed, and Percocet's left me hung-over and analyzing the events which took place. I actually slept with four different people in less than 24 hours. I feel like such a slut. My body aches and my coochie is sore. I've worked hard for money before, but last night honey, I put in heavy duty work! There was an envelope next to my pillow with Amber written on it. I opened it and realized it was five $500 Visa gift cards inside. Keke and Sonia woke up complaining about having headaches and not being able to remember a thing that took place. Somehow throughout the night I managed to dress their drinks with a memory loss supplement.

"Oh my God!" Sonia screamed. She held out her left hand and twirled around the room we all simultaneously ended up in. "Where is my engagement ring?" She asked frantically. Sonia began flipping pillows, mattresses, and sheets as she searched for her missing ring. "I wore it on the island. And I wouldn't have ever taken it off!" Keke and I looked puzzled as she went on a rampage trashing the room.

"Is everything okay in there ladies?" Keke went to open the door and Rachel appeared standing behind it with a concerned looked on her face.

"Yes. Well, we hope so. Sonia can't find her engagement ring and she was wearing it last night." Keke told her.

"Oh no honey! I hope you locate it because that ring is gorgeous!" Rachel said. Sonia, not paying any attention to Rachel, continued to look for the ring. "If I happen to run across it, I will notify you. I came over to invite you all to breakfast on the back patio. It's beautiful out. So once you ladies get fully dressed please join us outside in about an hour for some delicious food and mimosas." She handed Keke towels and three white uniforms through the crack of the door. "Good luck with the search hun," she said before closing the door behind her. Keke separated the towels from the plastic wrapped clothes and removed the uniforms from the packaging.

"Oh this is kind of cute." Keke said. It was a two piece shorts scrub set with Fantasy Connection embroidered on the front side of the top in blue. She handed Sonia and I ours just before trying hers on.

"Why are you two acting like my ring isn't of any importance or value?" Sonia asked out of frustration.

"I'm sure it's here somewhere Sonia. Calm down." I uttered.

"Are you kidding me, Syn? Terrence is going to kill me when he realizes I don't have it! The wedding is only next month and the wedding band is part of the engagement ring. It's a pair that we selected together." Sonia informed us as she wept.

"It's okay Sonia. We'll help you look for it." Keke said trying to comfort her.

"It has to be here! It just has to be!" Sonia started pacing the floor and talking to herself. "Ugh and I can't remember a got damn thing from last night! The last thing I remember is us sitting at the dinner table and I was twirling it around my finger." Sonia recalled.

"Maybe you removed it to avoid feeling some type of way just in case some acts of infidelity were to take place." I said as a suggestion.

"Screw you Syn! I wouldn't have ever removed my ring. No matter what!" Sonia yelled.

"I have a suggestion!" Keke said interrupting. "Let's all shower, get dressed, eat some breakfast and try to determine all of the possibilities then come back to the room and search again."

"I'm down for that." I told her.

"Sonia?" Keke looked over at Sonia for her approval.

"I suppose that's fine as long as we continue searching."

Once we'd gotten dressed we headed down the stairs through the kitchen and onto the patio. The sun shined brightly as the palm trees blew in the wind. Seagulls flew over the sand and ocean so gracefully. Three handsome gentlemen dressed in khaki pants and light blue Polo shirts escorted us to our seats. Our hotel was visible from their backyard. The early morning view of the white sand and the gorgeous blue water provoked us into the decision of taking a swim. Breakfast was arranged in a buffet style which was set up beautifully in honor of all of last night's remaining guests. Everyone sat around a huge bar with granite tops and high chairs which were extremely comfortable. The men served all of us bottled water and mimosas right before we headed towards the buffet.

The buffet consisted of fresh fruit, a variety of cereal, three choices of milk, juice, and flavored water. Omelets were prepared as they were ordered. There was pork and turkey bacon and sausage, grits, oatmeal, plenty of pastries, biscuits, waffles, as well as pancakes. As we ate the delicious food we were told that we would be shuttled back to our hotel in 3 hours. Rachel and Tony had outdoor men's and women's restrooms with beach towels, flip flops, personal items, and swimwear in various colors and sizes available for purchase.

"What do you feel like doing Sonia?" I asked her. She continued chewing her food with her head down.

"I don't want to get into anything before finding my ring." Sonia stated. Keke rubbed Sonia's back and gave her a side hug.

"Don't worry ladybug. We'll find it." Keke added.

"I will help you look for a little while then I would like to go for a quick swim." I told them.

"Syn you can be so insensitive sometimes. You can swim when we get back to our resort. Sonia needs us now."

"Yeah. I guess you're right!" I said to them. "Sonia do you have insurance on your ring?" I asked.

"I used to have it, but since Terrence has not been able to work as much, the upcoming wedding reception, and the non-stop medical bills, I decided not to renew it this year. The thing is, I have to be honest with you two." Keke and I both turned our bodies to face Sonia.

"What is it?" I asked first.

"You can talk to us about anything, Sonia. You should know that by now." Keke disclosed.

"We're already married." She revealed.

"What!?!" I yelled. Sonia and Keke acted surprised at my reaction to the news. "I mean what? How? When?" I wanted to know.

"For a while. He'd proposed years ago and that summer before he was diagnosed with cancer while we were visiting Las Vegas, we decided to get hitched. It was fun and spontaneous, but we were also sitting on top of the world then. He'd just gotten a promotion with his job at the marketing firm. I'd just won the honor of top Botanist in

Atlanta and life couldn't have been more perfect." She concluded.

"Wow. So why was it such a secret?" I asked her.

"We got married because we loved and respected each other. Our intentions were to hide it because of insurance and tax purposes. We knew that we would be having a wedding soon and didn't think too far into it. Now with the lack of communication, abuse, infidelity, and now the missing ring, I doubt if there will even be a wedding." Sonia sadly stated.

"What's so bad about that?" Keke asked. "Maybe there shouldn't be a wedding if he's mistreating you."

"The unfortunate thing about us being married is the prenuptial agreement we signed. I agreed to pay alimony if anything was to take place during or after our marriage on his behalf." She informed us. I finally realized what Terrence was doing. He wanted to set Sonia up for failure on purpose. Hmmmm. I wondered if getting Drake back is even worth the hassle.

"Everything will work itself out as it should Sonia. If we don't find the ring before we leave we can search for a similar ring at the jewelry shop in our hotel." I suggested.

"Are you kidding me Syn? That was a $20,000 engagement ring and it belonged to his great grandmother. I can't afford to replace it; not even with a replica!" Sonia cried aloud. One of the gentlemen rushed over to Sonia with a box of Kleenex tissues in hand. I grabbed a few and placed them in front of her then turned around and smiled at the young man to tell him thank you.

"Come on Sonia. Let's go upstairs and continue the hunt for this ring. It has to be here somewhere." Keke said while trying to console her. The two of them went back upstairs. I finished my meal and walked around the villa seeking Rachel. She has to have seen something with all of the surveillance she has around here. I figured if any of us could locate this ring, it would be her. While walking through the kitchen I overheard Rachel and Tony's voices coming from their office. I peeped through the slightly cracked door and saw a strange man holding what appeared to be Sonia's engagement ring under a microscopic lens.

"You're saying this is worth more than $10,000?" He asked them while twirling around in his chair.

"We figured it would be worth around that. It's an antique just like the one my great aunt had during the Civil War. There were only two created in the whole wide world by a jeweler who traveled across the world collecting various types of stones, diamonds, gems, crystals, gold, and silver." Tony informed him.

"Son this isn't it! This ring is only worth a few hundred bucks." He advised.

"A measly hundred bucks? The breakfast we served this morning is worth more than that!" Rachel said pissed.

"It's okay dear. It's better that I create a ring simply for you; one that is just as elegant and sleekly designed." Tony told her. "Now give this back to the poor lady before she drives herself nuts." He suggested. Rachel hugged Tony and kissed his cheek.

"Only for you Daddy." Rachel told Tony. I quietly backed away from the door and ran up the stairs to the guest room. Panting and unable to speak, as soon as I sat down on the bed to tell Sonia and Keke about what just happened, Rachel knocked on our door.

"Excuse me ladies, sorry to interrupt, but I have good news!" She said as she pulled Sonia's ring from her pocket. Sonia jumped over a pile of clothes that were in the center of the floor and ran over to Rachel grabbing the ring from her hand.

"Oh God thank you! Thank you Rachel! Thank you so much!" Sonia screamed. She was overwhelmed with joy and couldn't stop saying thank you. "Where was it?" Sonia asked.

"It was left on our bathroom counter near the sink. Tony brought it down to me, but we're not sure how it ended up there."

"It doesn't even matter! I'm delighted that you found it!" Sonia reiterated.

"Now that you're excited you ladies should get out and enjoy this weather. There's a volleyball net set up on the sand and a pool near the beach if you're not into getting any sand on you this early. The shuttle will be here in a couple of hrs. Enjoy while you still can."

"Thanks for the hospitality Rachel. We'll be back down soon." Keke said. Rachel left soon after and just as I decided to spill the information I'd obtained while snooping, I couldn't do it. I knew that it would disappoint Sonia to know that the ring she held close to her heart wasn't worth what she expected. I did however, want them to know not to trust Rachel and Tony, but since we'll be leaving here soon it almost didn't matter.

CHAPTER 11

Syndicate Intervention

Once we were relaxed and settled in our suite we began packing away the souvenirs we'd collected and sent our worn clothes to the cleaners. Sonia seemed extremely excited to be going home and Keke and I were feeling kind of down.

"This was the shortest vacation ever." Keke expressed. "Typically I only vacation a weekend when I visit my home town, but anytime I travel outside of the country I'm away at least a week."

"I apologize for ruining it for you two, but I need to get home to my baby and to my man." Sonia said.

"We aren't blaming you. We were expecting it to be a bittersweet moment when we booked the flights." I told her.

"She's right. I know you have a wedding to look forward to and I need to get back to finish up some work related matters. There are a few business things and clients I need to attend to prior to me flying in to Atlanta for your celebration.

Besides we needed this time to catch up and dabble into our wild sides before your big day." Keke said.

"Chile, she's already officially married." I mentioned.

"That may be true, but we will not be able to speak in front of others the way we did on this trip. Just wait and see. There will be family members she hasn't seen in a long time and colleagues you and I haven't spoken to in a while."

"Since we are departing early morning, we need to get out and do some last minute shopping." I said.

"Sure I'm down for a little shopping." Keke said agreeing.

"I'm going to hang out and do a little cleaning and packing for a while. You all can meet me on the beach when you're done." Sonia said.

"Are you sure?" I asked.

"Yes I want to stay in relaxation mode and continue reading this book I've neglected since our flight here." Sonia held up, "The Seven Spiritual Laws of Success," by Deepak Chopra.

"Oh this guy is amazing!" Keke said snatching the book from Sonia's hand.

"I read this book a few years ago during the summer break. I was battling myself about which career to pursue and it was in that moment of completing it that I decided to venture out and do art related teaching and private adult lessons." Keke said to us.

"You ladies are already successful. What could this book have provided for you that you didn't already know?" I asked out of curiosity.

"It helps you understand your overall purpose in life. The most important thing that stood out from the book for me is understanding how to direct your energy. It touches on having a choice to feel some type of way about something negatively or positively. It doesn't necessarily have to be received as it is intended to be received. We are able to control our mood, our beliefs, and our character by thinking before reacting. It's spiritually fulfilling." Keke shared.

"I will need to check it out when you're done boo."

"That's perfectly fine with me." Sonia said. Keke and I grabbed our purses and headed out the door. We walked into the boutiques downstairs before going into the casino to play on the slot machines. Keke grabbed a seat next to my slot machine.

"I've been thinking about what I would like to get them as a wedding gift." Keke said.

"What were you thinking?"

"I'm considering an all-expense paid honeymoon to Cabo San Lucas, Mexico." She said.

"That seems expensive, but I'm sure she and Terrence would love to share that moment away in peace!"

"Sonia definitely deserves it! I've already spoken to Terrence's mother and she's looking forward to keeping her grandson for a week or longer if she needs to."

"Really Keke? That's awesome! Sonia will be grateful!" I said.

"It is so shocking that we are all successful in our own way, but we are either hit or miss when it comes down to our love lives." Keke mentioned.

"You can say that again. I have no clue what I'm doing. I'm still in love with Drake's trifling ass, but I know there has to be a man who's meant for me. If he isn't wealthy or worthy in the bedroom I can't do anything with him."

"There is no better feeling than being spoiled by a mate who can also lay it down in the bedroom." Keke said.

"I agree. I don't know, it's as if I meet a man and he automatically assumes all I want is his money."

"Most of the time that is all you want Syn." Keke told me. "You are a gorgeous woman. You have a degree in Public Relations and you are in the process of getting your cosmetology license. Your problem is that you love broke thugs and wealthy old men. Neither of them can make you solely happy." I shook my head agreeing.

"I just want to be loved."

"No. I disagree with that. You're lonely and you haven't found yourself so you have chosen to settle for whatever the next best thing is at that particular time of need."

"I guess." I said. Keke looked me in my eyes.

"You're my girl, but that's how you've managed to build a bad reputation." She said.

"What is that supposed to mean?" I asked.

"It means that if someone hears about what you're all about before actually getting to know you then they will use you to their advantage. If you're acting like a wife you will get wifed, and well if you act loose, you get treated loosely. This game doesn't give a care about you and what you have to offer if the word whore has any relation to your name."

Keke said. "For instance, you know I have a wild side, but not too many other people do. I mean sure they are aware of my sexual orientation, but they can't say for sure what else I'm in to. Before respecting the game I respect myself and I have always been about my own damn money. The only way to make it in this world is to have your own shit to fall back on. Don't waste any time depending on others to make you or to provide you with resources you could have provided for your damn self."

"What do you propose I do first?" I asked.

"First you need to start praying and having faith that your life can be changed. You have always been known as a gold- digger, but if you start making your own money consistently, people have no choice but to start showing you respect. Once you've gained that power within, start changing up your image."

"What's wrong with my image?"

"Your image is perfect if you're attempting to remain in your same realm. However, if you want to be treated like a boss chic, you have to appear as such. Your nails are way too long and so are your extensions. Wear less makeup and switch up your wardrobe."

"My wardrobe too?!?" I questioned. "My wardrobe consists of the latest designer outfits and heels. Girlfriend you need to get with this." I told her.

"Designer fashions are fabulous to have when they are in season. The items that I've seen you wear within the last few days are almost considered vintage. The red bottoms are obviously worn and your clothes are either too large or too small. Take pride in your appearance and I guarantee you will feel much better about yourself and you will not take any bullshit from anyone."

"You're always trying to act as our older sister or something." I told Keke.

"Call it whatever you want, but I have always had you and Sonia's backs and I always plan to."

"Whoooooo!" I screamed! "Jackpot!" Engulfed with excitement I jumped out of my chair and started dancing. Keke joined in and we began doing the old school tootsie roll. Winning $5K couldn't have come at a better time.

"Let's go cash it in!" I said. "We're going shopping!"

"Not so fast little lady. Consider what we just discussed. Maybe you can think of some other things that are much more substantial than shopping right away." Keke said ruining the mood.

"What about my new wardrobe?" I asked.

"You can buy a few pieces, but you should invest that money into something else that will benefit you for the long haul."

"Okay Momma Kelis. We will do it your way." I said jokingly.

"At the end of the day it belongs to you and you have the right to do as you please." Keke said.

"If you were me, what would you spend it on?"

"I'd get the casino to cut me a cashier's check and make that decision once I get home after sorting through my bills and my future plans. Everything should be in order of importance. Things that can wait let it wait."Keke suggested.

"I will do that. Let's go check on Sonia and see how far she's gotten with packing." We finished our free drinks and cashed out. Keke and I ran into the chaperones we met the first day on the island.

"Hello! How have you all been enjoying your trip?" Keke asked them.

"It's been grand!" The gentleman shared. The other two said they were having a great time as well.

"That's wonderful! We will see you around!" I said.

"Have a goodnight!" Keke told them. As we were heading to unlock our door, we heard Sonia vomiting in the restroom near the front door. We rushed in to find her laying in her own puke.

"What happened Sonia?"

"Are you okay?" We asked her. Not being able to answer us immediately, Sonia hung her head back over the commode. Keke grabbed a towel from the counter and wet it with cold water before placing it on Sonia's forehead.

"I've been unable to keep any of my food down since you all left." Sonia stated as she wiped chunks of vomit from her mouth.

"It's okay we're here now." Keke assured her. We listened to music while we packed away our things. When we finished Keke decided to kick off story time since I interrupted her when she last attempted to share one of her sexual experiences.

"I have quite a few stories, but the one that interests me the most is Halloween 2012." Keke said.

"Tell us more." Sonia said. Keke looked over at me.

"Do you think you can handle it this time around Syn?" Keke asked.

"I promise not to say a word." I told her.

"We will see."

"Come on with it. I won't be rude this time." I said. Keke sat up on the sofa and began telling her story.

"I exited the elevator onto the 8th floor of her apartment building. As I slowly approached her door I paused before knocking. I heard music coming from inside. It corrupted my inner soul and I immediately felt aroused. I calmed myself down because we had a Halloween birthday party to attend." 'She's waiting for me,' I thought to myself. "Anticipating her strong arms wrapped around my soft body, I knocked on her door. I heard Ace bark from behind the closed door."

'Get back Ace!' "I heard her say before opening the door for me. She stood there wearing all black with a look on her face that was indescribable. I walked in and noticed the room was dim and filled with lit candles throughout the living area. I sat down on the couch and Ace came over to greet me."

'Hey Aceypooh!' I said excitedly. "He licked my face before Kaden told him to get down."

'How was your day?' "Kaden asked before passing me the blunt she'd rolled before my arrival."

'It was ok.' I responded. 'How was yours?'

'It was good.'

'Cool.' "I sat there next to her wanting her to make a move. It was something about her lips and her touch that instantly soaked my panties. As we passed the weed back and forth, I looked over in her direction and she was in the process of coming in for a kiss. I melted. My heart raced and my kitty was damn near crying for her to say hello. Our tongues collided and before I knew what I was doing, I'd climbed on top of her."

'Why are you playing?' Kaden asked. 'You know we have this party to go to.'

'Playing? Who said I was playing? They can wait.'

"I ripped her sleeveless shirt from her body and sucked on her neck. I wanted her to touch my kitty so bad I couldn't take it anymore. Forcing her hand up my skirt I pulled my panties to the side before placing the palm of her hand on the lips of my kitty. It was so wet her entire palm was infused with so much moisture she was sliding up and down without attempting to."

'Come inside.' I whispered in her ear. "She was grinding the bottom half of her body and biting her lips. I knew she wanted to come inside, but she loved teasing me. It was too late; I was beyond ready for her to fuck me. I didn't even care how or with what I just needed to be penetrated and quickly. Moving her hand down to my entrance, I managed to put two of her fingers in me and I started riding them."

'Damn!' she shouted. 'What the hell are you trying to do to me?'

'I'm trying to make you fall in love.' I said playfully and sexually.

'Nah, don't do that.'

'Don't do that? Why not? You said you love my pussy right?' I asked as I hopped up and down on her fingers while kissing her neck. "She was so turned on and I knew it was the perfect opportunity to seduce her, but before I could work my magic, she pulled down her sweatpants and popped out her piece, and I loved her strap! I was actually in love with it. My breaths became less faint and my moans grew intensely."

'You ready for some Johnson?' Kaden asked abruptly. "The exchange of passion we shared was almost too much to turn down, but we had to get to the party. I kissed her passionately before hopping off."

'I'll get it when we get back tonight.' "I smiled at her as she walked in the restroom to change.

Later that evening we arrived back at her place after enjoying the festivities. The vinyl cat suit I changed into was fitting like I'd just gotten dressed for the evening, but due to the smell of whip cream and chocolate on me from the human sundae I created for the birthday girl, I decided to shower. As I washed my body with Dove soap and Dahlia Noir by Givenchy bath gel, Kaden knocked on the bathroom door. Before I could respond, she peeped her head into the bathroom and I told her to come right in. She entered as I continued to wash myself, and turned off the bathroom lights. I opened the shower curtain just enough to see what she was up to. Kaden stood there wearing her strap and nothing else. My mouth fell open as I took in the silhouette of her sexy ass body. Even though the room was dark, I was able to see her. She joined me and I began washing her back with my cloth and soaping the rest of her body with my other hand. Kaden embraced me before kissing my neck. The tunes of Marques Houston's song, 'Naked' played in the background. I grabbed the back of her head moving her lips closer to mine before kissing her. I blushed as she stood in front of me with nothing but skin. The sounds of the music set the mood perfectly. Our moans overlapped as she stuck her fingers in my snatch."

'Why are you so wet?' she whispered softly in my ear.

'You did that!' I said breathing heavily. 'You always make me so wet!' "She pushed me against the wall of the shower and forced my thighs apart before coming deeper inside of me."

'Fuck me!' I screamed. 'Fuck me, Baby! I need you now!' "My right hand gripped her dreads as she dug inside of me. I turned around and bent over facing the bottom of the tub as she entered me from behind. Filled with lust and an overwhelming feeling of passion, we made love like we never wanted it to end. The water from the shower head ran down my back onto my ass making it very slippery and wet. My moans grew louder and louder. She covered my mouth with her hand making my sexual announcements faint. Suddenly I got the urge to pee. I didn't want to tell her anything because I didn't want her to stop pleasing me."

'What's wrong?' she asked. Hesitating I answered, 'I need to pee.'

'So pee,' she replied. "The thought of peeing on her fascinated me. I'd never peed on anyone else before, but I felt so liberated and free at that moment. My body grew numb and I couldn't do anything. Kaden smacked my ass before exiting my kitty and sat on side of the tub. I stood over her and played with my clit in an attempt to give her the golden shower she requested. Kaden changed the water to a much cooler temperature. It gave me the sensation and urge of wanting to pee even more. Before I knew it, I came and peed on her thighs."

'Yeah baby cum for me,' she yelled out in excitement. "I screamed like never before. My moans and trembling body were uncontrollable." Keke placed one of throw pillows from the sofa in between her legs. "Maybe I need to stop here because I'm getting mad horny." She revealed.

"You lil nasty trick." I said jokingly. Both Keke and Sonia laughed along.

"That wasn't too bad was it Syn?" Sonia asked.

"Nah it wasn't so bad."

"You sure do have a thing for dreadlocks." Sonia mentioned.

"And I always will." Keke explained smiling. The remainder of our evening consisted of resting and making sure Sonia was okay.

CHAPTER 12

Back to Reality

Sonia had a difficult time on our flight back, but she seemed well when Terrence and Jaxon picked us up from the airport. She embraced Jaxon when he ran into her arms.

"Mommy mommy! I missed you so much mommy!" Jaxon carried on as we walked to claim our baggage.

"Well hello Terrence." Sonia said as she put Jaxon down to hug his father.

"What's up baby? How was your trip?" He inquired.

"It was good. I missed you." Sonia said to him.

"Cool." He responded.

"What's good big head?" Terrence said to me.

"Nothing much little head." I told him. With a half smirk on his face I knew he understood which head I was referring to. We located our luggage then Terrence and Sonia dropped me home first. There were two packages on my door step and a dozen of red roses with a small envelope attached. I opened it only to find a note which read: *"Stopped by... hit me up when you get this... Love, Drake."* Here we go with his bullshit I thought to myself. My cell phone rang before I could unlock the front door completely. I glanced at it and noticed it was an incoming call from a restricted phone number.

"Hello?" I answered.

"Did you get the flowers I left you?" Drake spoke.

"Yes. I'm actually just getting in. Would you mind calling me back in about an hour?" I responded.

"Yeah whatever yo!" He said before disconnecting the line. After rolling my luggage inside and placing my packages down on the coffee table I checked messages on my answering machine which were mostly from clients wanting to make hair appointments. The overpowering stench coming from the kitchen caught my attention. I should have taken my trash out before leaving because it smelled disgusting! This will be the last time I ever leave tilapia behind in the garbage. I unlatched the deadbolt to my backdoor and an injured cat was clinging for life on the bottom of my step. It appeared to have been attacked by a wild animal. I googled the animal control number and called them to come over. It wasn't long before they arrived with a crate to remove the kitten from my back yard. Finally after dealing with the cat, cleaning my kitchen, and reaching out to clients, I was able to come up with a suitable investment plan. While completing cosmetology school, I've decided to provide a more professional and comfortable environment for my regular clients. My back bedroom isn't being used for anything except storage and Drakes clothes that he left behind. I walked to the back of room to take measurements. The colors and design ideas I had in mind encouraged me to execute my plan into action. I began searching for the necessities for a small and intimate home salon. I'd been so engulfed with the ideas that were running through my mind I'd forgotten to check out the packages that were left outside my door. I poured a glass of Italian Amarone and walked over to the table. One of the envelopes consisted of a hair magazine subscription and the other one was an unlabeled DVD. The outside of the envelope hadn't been labeled either. I turned on my television and popped the disc into the DVD player. The room looked very familiar and it wasn't until I heard the audio of myself moaning that I damn near spit out my wine. There I was on my back getting head from some nameless woman while Tony's penis hung down my throat. How in the hell did this get here? I wondered. My moans were painful to hear. I watched as I gagged on him and seemed to be enjoying the female participant. Failing at the attempt to remember the acts that were taking place on screen I immediately dialed Keke's phone. Then I thought about her knowing about my woman to woman interaction so I quickly hung up. This can't be real. Who would send this? A feeling of helplessness overcame me and it hindered my spirit and I immediately had no control over my thoughts. It was extremely uncomfortable and all of the future improvements I had planned for my business were instantly forgotten. Keke returned my call during mid thought.

"Hey girl!" I answered attempting not to sound bothered.

"Hey lady! Is everything okay?" She asked.

"Yes I was checking to see if you'd made it home by now." I lied.

"Not quite. I have a layover in North Carolina and then I'm off to Dallas."

"Aww well text me once you're settled."

"Okay hun... will do." She said.

Searching for answers in my mind, I couldn't think of one thing from that night. I continued to watch the film as it transitioned into another scene. I rode Tony while eating the young lady. I caught a quick glimpse of her and realized it was, Sonia! This has to be a setup! It's such a disgrace! I couldn't continue watching. I removed the DVD from the DVD player and broke it into tiny pieces before flushing them down the toilet. I do not understand how this even got back to the states so soon. Nothing is adding up to me. I can't reach out to either of my friends without telling them the entire story and I'm too ashamed to admit that I drugged them, but apparently I could have possibly been drugged as well and that means that I slept with a total of five different people. My eyes began to tear up and I decided to pour myself another glass of wine and run a hot bubble bath hoping to gain clarity from our weekend getaway.

CHAPTER 13

Wedded Bliss

Sonia and Terrence decided that there was no other way to celebrate their union without emulating the fondness Sonia has for plants. Their wedding was being held in the evening at Atlanta's Botanical Garden. Sonia always dreamt of her wedding theme being somewhat of an enchanted garden which is why she selected Cascades garden to receive the look and feel she has desired. Last I heard she and Terrence have been doing well since we returned from the Bahamas. Drake and I are back together and Keke has reconnected with one of her college girlfriends whom she brought along as her date.

"There's rain in the forecast, but it's a super sunny day!" Sonia's mother stated while having her makeup applied.

"Mother I have stressed the entire week about there being a 60% chance of precipitation on today, but I have faith that the forecast will remain as is until the completion of the ceremony." Sonia said confidently.

"You look so stunning!" I told Sonia before tucking a blue hairpin in the back of her bun. She commenced to crying as Keke and I shared the wedding gifts we customized for her. We pitched in together and purchased a spa basket, filled with her favorite Bond No. 9 Hamptons perfume and candle set, Shalimar shower gel by Guerlain Paris, luxury skin care products by Clinique, a Victoria's Secret white lace baby doll, the honeymoon package to Mexico, and the totality of 6 spa salon visits to Bliss.

"Ladies you two are making me shed tears like a big baby. I'm going to ruin my makeup." Sonia pulled us closely and gave us both huge hugs. Someone knocked on the bridal room door signaling for us to get into our designated places. Sonia took a few deep breaths before shouting, "Let's do this!" The matron of honor asked us all to hold hands before leading us through a brief prayer just before exiting the room. Sonia's wedding colors were cream, white, and black. Her wedding dress was an off white long fitting Pnina Tornai lace gown cut low down the back with a black ribbon tied around her waist with a diamond and pearl brooch attached in the center. She wore her hair in a bun topped with a lace and pearl jeweled bird cage head piece. The makeup artist gave Sonia a 20's era makeover with light colored eyes and bright red lips. As Keke and I walked down the aisle we smiled at each other when we noticed that Sonia incorporated the bling covered mason jars we created in college together and used them as hanging candle holders. Tree lights, typically used on Christmas trees, were disbursed throughout the garden in an intricate way. Surrounded mostly by orchids, it was one of the most beautiful weddings I'd ever attended. There were an array of tropical plants and several fountains of water which created an elegant, romantic, and tranquil touch. Everyone present oohed and awed as Sonia approached the beginning of the aisle. Their son Jaxon escorted her. He looked adorably handsome wearing an all-black tuxedo which matched his dad's tux perfectly.

The song Pink Sky by H-town started to play as they headed towards the altar.

I woke up this morning

so happy

smell in the air of the sweet perfume you left in my room ohhh yeahh

you make me so happy lady

but you're gonna be my bride soon

oh ohhh

you are my shining star

the one that's around when my world's
crumbling down when the rain wash away my crown

all I gotta do is look up high

there's my pink sky

yeah yeah yeah yeah

pink sky

the color of sweet give life to the trees

pink sky

all around me yeah

my pink sky

yeah

a flower a virtue

no one else above you

your heaven is my love

so high I must pray to touch

yes God has made perfect one

in you this he has done

inside you're like fine wine

fine wine

priceless with no time

so long I've been waiting

for this special blessing

the woman of my dreams

and now it's reality

you're my star

the way you come around when I'm down
girl you lift my frown

I just look up and see my pink sky

my pink sky

the birds have to fly your air

pink sky

I love it when you're right there for me baby

(adlib)

I love you baby

yes I do

yeah yeah

nobody could ever take your place

you're my you're my you're my pink sky

I love you baby always ways ways

I wanna be right there when you need me

I love my my pink sky

you're my pink sky

"Please be seated." Minister Gavin said to the congregation. Jaxon stood in place after kissing his mother's hand before she approached Terrence. They held hands as the officiant began the opening remarks.

"Dearly beloved, we are gathered here today to witness the union of Terrence Coleman and Jacksonia Bradshaw in holy matrimony, which is an honorable estate, that is not to be entered into unadvisedly or lightly, but reverently and into this estate these two persons present come not to be joined. If anyone can show just cause why they may not be lawfully joined together, let them speak now or forever hold their peace." He paused momentarily awaiting a possible objection to their matrimony. "Who gives this woman to be married to this man?" Minister Gavin questioned.

"I do!" Jaxon announced loudly as he raised his hand. The guests burst out into laughter. Once the crowd calmed down Minister Gavin continued.

"Terrence and Sonia are here to express their very own words, feelings, and intent of what will bind them as one. So at this time I call upon them to speak their wishes before you all; the vows that will unite them forever."

Terrence kicked it off by saying, "Sonia, baby, I love you with every muscle in my body. Your drive, commitment, effort, and desire to impose love on everything you encounter is my strength and motivation to survive. It gives me courage to live everyday as if it were my last. I will spend the rest of our lives seeking more ways to love you better. Sonia you deserve the world and I intend on providing you with the best life God enables me to give. You are my queen, my heartbeat, and the nourishment of my soul. I am forever and always yours."

"Awwwww!" everyone said as he finished.

"Terrence you've introduced me to many things, but most importantly, you're the bravest man I've ever known. When you were sick and I wasn't too sure how to succumb to the reality of what was taking place you held me together; simply put I was in disarray. During your weakest moment you were my vigor and light to a brighter outcome. Your inclination to live and continue to be here for Jaxon and I proved that you subjected the deepest of your love, emotions, and strength into us. Terrence you have sacrificed for your families' sake, and for that I give you all of me. I promise never to leave your side through sickness, financial strain, the potential harm of a devil's advocate, or anything that may attempt to hinder our family, our relationship, our bond, or our future. Today I say to you in front of our friends and family, I have always been about you; then, now, forever and always." Sonia said in tears. The congregation made their sentimental remarks again. Minister Gavin turned to Terrence and continued the ceremony.

Sonia and Terrence exchanged rings then Minister Gavin looked at them both and said, "You may now share your first kiss as husband and wife." Terrence grabbed Sonia's face and pulled her closer to him. They locked lips like a pair of high school kids who were making out while their parents were away from home.

"Ladies and gentlemen, I present to you Mr. and Mrs. Coleman." Minister Gavin announced. The congregation threw authentic white rose petals at them as they walked down the aisle hand in hand as the rest of us followed. Terrence and Sonia provided their wedding party with a Hummer H2 limousine to chauffeur us to Piedmont Park for wedding photos while they trailed behind in a horse and carriage. Surprisingly the rain held up even with the clouds. We were able to take plenty of photos and head back to the venue to partake in the reception. The wedding planner introduced the wedding party before Sonia and Terrence made their entrance.

"Please stand and make a lot of noise for the newlyweds; Mr. and Mrs. Terrence G. Coleman!" Everyone gave the couple a standing ovation. Sonia and Terrence took to the floor to have their first dance. Everything seemed to be moving along as scheduled making it a smoother transition into the rest of the evening.

Chapter 14

Wedding Day Chaos

Keke and I made a toast then the wedding coordinator played a video slideshow of the bride and groom. Moments later I looked over at Sonia and I noticed her facial expression change in an instant. Observing the screen carefully I realized it was the same video I played in my living room over a month ago. Everyone looked intrigued and suddenly uninterested in finishing their salmon and chicken dishes. My heart dropped down to my stomach as I perceived the pain Sonia was feeling as well as the anger Terrence was emulating. Promptly standing to his feet, Terrence grabbed Sonia by her bun lifting her from her seat.

"What the fuck is this?" He asked screaming at her.

"I don't know! I don't know what's going on!" She responded hastily. The smirk he projected afterwards clearly meant he was done. Everyone around us was appalled by the occurrence of the unexpected events. Terrence walked out angrily while the wedding coordinator attempted to remove the video from the screen. She finally managed to stop the amateur porn that exhibited me, Sonia, and Tony getting it on, but by then the guests were too aware of the shenanigans which had taken place during our mini weekend vacation. The older women were whispering back and forth. Mothers of young children struggled to cover their eyes. The men were laughing and carrying on while Sonia crawled under the dinner table and curled up like a fetus as she cried her heart out.

"Take my hand Sonia! Let's get out of here!" Keke told her before grabbing her hand. Sonia followed us to our dressing room. We ran in latching the door behind us.

"What the hell just happened?" Sonia cried out.

"I'm trying to figure out the same exact thing." Keke stressed. "Did you know anything about this?" She asked looking at me. I put my head down partially embarrassed.

"Yes! I mean no!" I said.

"Trick which is it? Either you did or you didn't!" Keke yelled.

"No!" I screamed. "Not like that." I pleaded. Sonia walked over to me and slapped me.

"It was you! It was you all along!" Sonia screamed. I held my face in disbelief.

"I had nothing to do with this! I promise!" I pleaded.

"A few months ago I noticed your number on Terrence's phone records and I gave you the benefit of the doubt hoping the two of you were planning something for he and I. Keke was right! You're nothing but a lying ratchet slut bitch!" She told me aggressively. "I hate you!" Sonia screamed. "Get this whore out of my face!" She demanded. "I hate you!" She expressed. Keke walked over separating the two of us.

"Syn look at me! Did you know anything about this?" Keke asked trying to get me to reveal what she wanted to know. Crying and shocked at everything that was occurring I began to explain.

"Someone sent the same video in an un-addressed envelope to my home last month on the same day we returned from the Bahamas." I revealed.

"Why didn't you say anything to us?" Keke asked.

"Because I didn't remember and I was embarrassed that this even happened. I never wanted you two to know that I slept with another woman; especially not either of you! But I promise I had nothing to do with what just happened!" I yelled crying and pleading. All of a sudden someone came knocking at the door aggressively.

"Jacksonia are you in there honey?" Sonia's mom yelled through the door.

"Go away mother!" Sonia told her. She continued knocking on the door frantically. "Not now mother!" Sonia screamed.

"It's important honey! Open up please!" She pleaded.

"Mom I said to go away!" Sonia reiterated.

"Jaxon is missing dammit!" She informed her. Sonia immediately walked over to the door and opened it.

"What are saying mother? Are you saying my baby isn't with you?" Sonia asked overly concerned.

"No I left him outside for a short while to play with the other children, but when I noticed his other little cousins were back inside without him I began to worry. I asked all of them where Jaxon is and they have no clue."

"You were supposed to keep an eye on him mother!" Sonia kicked her heels off slinging them across the floor. She quickly slipped on her sneakers and snatched her purse. Slightly shoving her mother out of her way, Sonia led the way in search of Jaxon while the three of us chased her. Sonia ran outside and looked down one end of the street then back to the other side of the street. We searched the restrooms and the playground area positioned in the back of the venue and Jaxon was nowhere in sight. Sonia power walked over to the area where the Dj settled and grabbed his microphone.

"Excuse me everyone. I apologize for the disorderly conduct and the inappropriate behavior which took place earlier, but at this moment I am unable to locate my son Jaxon. He is currently missing. Has anyone seen or heard anything that could be helpful to us locating him?" Most of them shook their heads saying no. "I'm asking all of you who are mobile to please assist us in finding him." Sonia said as she wept. The guests quickly scattered throughout the venue to help with the search of Jaxon. Sonia's mother, Ms. Lee, called 911 to alert them of the news.

"My grandson missing!" She said frenzied. "Tell them you need to put out an amber alert!" I told her.

"They told me tell you Amber alert!" She spoke. "Uh, he say no proof of abduction, no alert!" She informed us. Due to Ms. Lee's accent and lack of understanding, Keke seized the phone and began to speak with the 911 operator.

"Hello ma'am! Is there any way we can maybe put out an Amber Alert for the missing child?" Keke asked waiting for the operator to respond. "But he's only three years old. His name is Jaxon and he was outside playing with his cousins and he went missing. We don't have any additional details." Keke looked agitated while trying to convince the 911 operator to alert everyone about Jaxon. She moved the receiver away from her mouth. "They're saying that they can only issue an Amber Alert if there's proof that the child has been abducted or is at risk of serious injury or death." Sonia snatched the phone from Keke's hands.

"Hello! Listen Ms. Operator. My son is no place to be found. There aren't any clues leading me straight to him. I am asking law enforcement to help me out in any way possible." Sonia requested. "24 hours?!? He's a toddler, and although he's very intelligent for his age, he's still a young child for God's sake! I can't believe you bastards are telling me to wait an entire 24 hours!" Sonia howled before disconnecting the line. "I'll acquire my baby's whereabouts by my damn self!" Sonia stressed.

"I'll call Terrence and make sure Jaxon isn't with him." Sonia looked over at me then rolled her eyes.

"Yes you go right along whore." She said to me. Ignoring her, I dialed his number and he picked up.

"Hello Terrence. Is Jaxon with you?" I inquired.

"No. Why?" He asked. Sonia suddenly snatched the phone from my hand and placed it on speaker phone.

"He's missing Terrence! Our baby is missing!" She cried out.

"Wait. What? I thought he was with Ms. Lee." Terrence responded.

"He was, but now we aren't sure where he is." Sonia informed him. "You need to come back and help us search for our baby boy."

"I don't have to do shit! That's you and your mom's responsibility. When I left there he was in the company of your family. So miss me with all that nonsense. You better find him too!" Terrence demanded just before hanging up on Sonia.

"Ughhhhhhh!" Sonia screamed. "This is so frustrating!" She removed her bird cage head piece and threw it against the wall. "That's it! I'm going to the police station and demanding that they find my son!" Sonia slid out of her wedding gown then ran to the closet that was designated for her and unzipped a garment bag and pulled out this beautiful silk white peplum jumper with appliqués and bling on the bodice. "Maybe if I appear as if I'm wealthy they'll care enough to assist me!" she shouted.

"Not right Sony! Not right!" Her mother added. Sonia cried while unpinning her hair and brushing down the bun she wore. She wiped her tears then applied a deep dark matte red colored lipstick. Grabbing her Roberto Cavalli cat eye sunglasses she headed towards the front door. "It's imperative that I find my baby and I won't stop until I do!" Sonia stated confidently before running out of the room leaving us behind. Sonia pushed through the crowd of dancing guests who decided to continue celebrating in spite of the missing child. We caught up with her as she approached the doors leading outside. Our eyes lit up instantly after noticing Jaxon only a few feet away from the front door of the venue. All of us began jumping up and down relieved that Jaxon was in plain sight's view. Mysteriously appearing out of nowhere, Jaxon sat on a tree stump near the waterfall. Sonia sprinted towards him dropping her car keys and clutch along the way. She picked him up into her arms and twirled him around as she kissed him all over his face. Jaxon, still wearing his tuxedo from earlier, held on to the back of his mother's neck. We ran over to them in tears and released an enormous sigh. Sonia's mother popped his backside with her hand.

"Jaxon what happened to you?" she asked him.

"I went to McDonalds with my friends!" He said excitedly pointing at the toy which came from his McDonald's kid's meal box which had fallen to the ground.

"McDonald's?" Sonia asked placing him back down. "Which friends Jaxon? All of your friends were here while you were missing."

"I wasn't missing Mommy. I left with Ms. Journey and the twins."

"You left with who!?!" Sonia yelled while shaking Jaxon by his arms.

"Mommy you're hurting me." Jaxon indicated.

"You are not allowed to go anywhere with strange people unless your father or myself have approved of it." I felt kind of bad because I thought back to Sonia revealing suspicious activities of Terrence while we were in The Bahamas and the name *Journey* rang a bell. Sonia looked Jaxon in his eyes and stated, "Listen I am happy that you're okay, but do not disappear ever again!" Jaxon held his head down.

"Yes ma'am." He replied. Sonia pulled him along by his arm and packed everything in her car.

"I'm going home. Tell everyone I apologize and explain how grateful I am of their attendance. Also, let everyone know that I will return their gifts over the next few weeks." Sonia told us.

"That's kind of rude Sonia."

"What is?" She asked.

"To tell the guests you will be returning their gifts. It may offend them."

"I'm sure it will offend them if I hold on to them." She persuaded us. "You know what. Just tell them whatever you ladies want to inform them. I'm out of here." Sonia stated before driving off. It began to storm as soon as we re- entered the building.

"I hope she's okay to drive." Keke said concerned as we watched Sonia's car eventually disappear.

Chapter 15
Lost for Words

Sonia's phone rang as she pulled off in a hurry.

"Hello?" she answered.

"Did you find my boy?" Terrence asked Sonia.

"Yes. He's here with me." Sonia informed him.

"Well where the hell was he?" Terrence asked.

"Jaxon! Cover your ears for a moment until Mommy tells you to uncover them." Jaxon obeyed his mother and placed his hands over his ears and she continued to converse with Terrence. "He was with that ugly, unpleasant, uneducated whore of yours!" Sonia stressed.

"Who? Tina? Mo' Nae? Veronica? Anita? Brenda? Rebecca? Stephanie? Hell which one of my hoes had my son with her?" He spoke sarcastically.

"This is not the time for one of your antics Terrence! I don't want any of those whores around my child!" She screamed.

"My nearly divorced wife has some nerve to have expectations. You were too busy fucking two other people on an amateur film that was exposed to all of our people! Get the fuck out of here with *your* bullshit. It's on now baby. You can't tell me shit ever again in life!" He shared. Sonia pulled the receiver closer to her mouth.

"You listen to me you little fuck boy! I don't care what you do from this point on, but I will go to war behind my son!" Sonia admitted.

"Suck my dick bitch! You want to know who he was with? He was with this bad ass chocolate shawty of mine named Journey. Yeah that damn Journey is the truth. Nice body, perfect juicy booty, she can cook, hold it down, and she sucks dick like she went to school for that shit, but most importantly she carried my twins." Terrence revealed. Outraged by what he was saying, Sonia was unable to speak. Her phone fell from her trembling hand onto the floor of the passenger side of her car. She gasped for oxygen as she reached for the fallen phone. Sonia increased her speed while swerving in and out of traffic attempting to get to Terrence as rapidly as possible.

"You stay your ass right there Terrence! We'll be there soon." She said yelling towards the phone. Sonia continued to speed in her Black Infiniti Q50. Jaxon removed his hands from his ears.

"Mommy! Mommy! Slow down!" He yelled. Sonia didn't pay him any mind. Jaxon began to weep as Sonia drove faster. Frightened by his mother's behavior, he screamed, "Mommy I'm scared!"

"It's okay Jaxon! We're almost home! I need you to sit back and be a big boy for Mommy." Jaxon looked around confused. "Can you do that for Mommy?" She asked looking through her rear view mirror.

"Okay Mommy. I can do it!" Jaxon said excitedly. Immediately as Sonia turned back around she hit a pothole and swerved her car to avoid hitting a homeless guy who was crossing the busy intersection and lost control of her vehicle. Running straight into a large oak tree the car came to a halt ejecting Jaxon from his car seat and causing Sonia to hit her head and blackout.

Two weeks later Sonia woke up in a panic.

"Where's my baby?" she asked frantically. The nurses attempted to calm her down as she struggled to remove the IV's from her arm. "What is all of this? Where's my son?" she screamed at everyone surrounding her.

"Mrs. Coleman, you and your son were in a horrible car accident. Unfortunately, he passed away a few days ago while you were in a coma." One of the nurses revealed. Sonia screamed so loud nothing else came out. The nurses gathered around her bed to console her.

"Your mother and a couple of friends are in the waiting room. Would you like me to get anyone?" One of the nurses offered.

"Nooooooo! I want Jaxon!" Sonia held her wrapped head. "Owww!" she yelled.

"Calm down Mrs. Coleman. You have a concussion and we're still running tests on you to make sure you're okay." Another nurse added.

"Okay?" Sonia questioned. "I will never be okay without my baby boy. I want my baby!" Sonia continued to scream. "Where is he? I want to see him right now!" she cried loudly. "My baby is too much of a joy to have died this soon. Where is my child?"

"He's right next to you Mrs. Coleman." The taller nurse said pointing to the gold urn that was placed on the table next to her hospital bed. Immediately becoming angry, Sonia started punching her face. Startled by her behavior, the nurses were somewhat unprepared. Afraid of what she'd do next they all moved closer to her to hold her hands down for her own protection.

"Who did that to my baby?" she screamed. "Did you do that to him? Did you do it?" She asked staring into the eyes of the nurses around the room. "I wouldn't have wanted that for my child!" Sonia cried.

"Your husband made the decision to have him cremated Mrs. Coleman." One of the ladies explained. Sonia began to cry vehemently.

"Why would he do this?" Sonia asked. Everyone continued to console her. Once calm, Sonia asked all of the nurses to leave. She rolled over on her side and faced the urn which carried Jaxon's remains.

Chapter 16

Today's Sorrows, Tomorrow Follows

Sonia was released from the hospital several weeks later. She'd gotten so thin and fragile she was hardly recognizable. The doctors were feeding her through a tube because she wouldn't eat on her own. Sonia blamed herself for Jaxon's death and attempted to take her own life on several occasions while admitted into the hospital. After further evaluation and prescription medication she was released to return home under special supervision.

Keke and I greeted Sonia and Ms. Lee with balloons, flowers, and teddy bears as they pulled up to Sonia's place. Terrence moved all of his things out and exhausted their savings account during her hospital stay.

"Hi ladies!" Ms. Lee said waving to us as she gathered Sonia's belongings while the home health nurse pushed Sonia in a wheelchair. We hugged Sonia and kissed her on the forehead as she entered the foyer of her home.

"It may not be a good time for visiting ladies. She's just taken her meds and she really needs to get some rest."

The home health nurse said to us.

"Aww, but we wanted to check on our girl." Keke told her. "I'm only in town for a few more days."

"Come back tomorrow." Ms. Lee added. "Tomorrow better."

"We can do that Ms. Lee." I said. We placed the gifts in the kitchen and left the house.

"Did you see the way Sonia was looking?" Keke asked. Sonia's face had sunken in, in such a short period of time.

"Unfortunately I did."

"It's so sad. Everything that has happened over the last two months is so surreal. How does one go from having the time of their lives on vacation, a perfect wedding day to such a horrible tragedy?" Keke stated.

"I know. Poor Jaxon, he loved his parents so much! They didn't deserve any of it." I said.

"Sonia didn't deserve to have you sleeping with her man behind her back either. She confided in me and expressed that she knew you and Terrence were sleeping together." She disclosed. I sighed before speaking.

"Well, um there's no proof that we've ever done anything." I said to her.

"Hold it Syn! It's me, Keke that you're speaking to. You can't bullshit a bullshitter."

"Okay okay. Between you and me, I've been holding a grudge towards Sonia all this time because she set me up with her home boy Karter in college."

"And what's wrong with trying to hook your girl up?" Keke asked.

"Nothing is wrong with introducing your friend to a nice young man, but he was the complete opposite of nice." I told her.

"How?" Keke asked.

"He is the reason I have ongoing trust issues. Karter took full advantage of me on our first date and when I told Sonia about it, she laughed and said my story didn't add up and for me to quit slandering his name. She said that he was too much of an intellectual genius and a gentleman who could have any woman that would have him. We had a huge fight and stopped speaking to one another for a good while."

"Oh, I remember that, but neither of you wanted to discuss what happened." She said.

"Yes that's exactly what had taken place."

"So did you file a police report?" she asked me.

"Yes, but I didn't go see a doctor until days later and I'd showered over 20 times. As her close friend I was offended by her not believing me."

"Well maybe she was close to him as well." Keke stated.

"They were close alright. Karter happens to be Terrence's first cousin. She and Karter dated briefly during undergrad, but I don't believe she slept with him.

"Why would you date her leftovers?" Keke asked me. "I wouldn't want to date anyone either of you or any of my other girlfriends have dated or slept with. It's just against girl code. You can date friends, but not your friend's lovers." She rambled.

"Sonia insisted. She told me that he was a very well-mannered young man who was studying to be a chemist. She kept going on about how great of a husband he would make and how beautiful our children would be." I informed her. "He was gentle over the phone, but in person it was as if he had something to prove."

"No offense, but maybe she could have possibly been considering your reputation." Keke mumbled.

"He sexually assaulted me! I don't give a damn what you or anyone else has to say about it. You just don't make up things like that. Listen, weeks before she introduced us, she was stressing over a midterm project which required specific research. I'm not too certain of all the details, but I know it had something to do with a drug called Rohypnol."

"Are you referring to the date rape drug?" Keke asked.

"Yes." I confirmed.

"How did you figure that?"

"Well, he and I had gone out to shoot pool at a local tavern. We ate and had a few drinks before taking a stroll in the park. When we walked back to the car he offered me an orange Sunkist soda and I took a sip of it. I remember us kissing and I'm not sure what happened in between the kiss and me waking up very sore the following morning in my dorm room." Keke gave me a suspicious stare. "I know what you're thinking, but it was a different kind of sore. I was raped and my best friend is part responsible for it; all for a good grade."

"Damn. It's almost too hard to consider that Sonia would do such a thing, but I'm sorry that happened to you. I can see why you've held on to it for this long, but it's time to let it go. I think karma has played its part in her life." Keke said.

"Yeah you're right. This is something that has followed me for years. It seems like since he and I got together I've run into bad boys."

"What ever happened to this Karter guy?"

"He's still around. He finished school and now he runs one of Atlanta's largest drug cartels. He's known around as King Karter."

"How long has it been since you've seen him?" Keke inquired.

"I saw him at the wedding. He was the one in the all black wearing shades sitting with my home girl Joy, the petite light skinned chic."

"Who is she?" Keke inquired.

"Joy is his lady. She's been down with him since the beginning. The poor girl was enrolled in cosmetology school with me, but one day he beat her so bad she couldn't attend class for a few weeks and she eventually dropped out. I guess she's better off letting him take care of her anyway." I explained.

"That's a bad move if that's what she's chosen to do." Keke said.

"Yeah well everyone isn't as fortunate as some of us." Immediately getting annoyed by our conversation I stopped talking and turned up the volume on my stereo. Keke asked me to drop her off to her hotel so that she wouldn't need to Uber from my place. Later that evening I had a moment to reflect on the decisions I'd made in my past that are still negatively affecting me today. I didn't want to be the person I'd become anymore. I wanted more; to be better. Life is too short.

I lit candles and incense, before getting on my knees to thank God for all that he has blessed me with as well as the things he denied me to have.

"God, I know we haven't spoken in a while, but I need you Lord. You are the only one who knows my heart. Most of the time my intentions are well, and sometimes they are not. (Chuckles) ...I can't even do wrong without feeling horrible about it. Please bless me with a forgiven heart. Free my mind from negative affirmations, evil provoking thoughts, and hate. Lord I ask that you make me over into a new woman. Create in me a pure heart and mind. Please forgive me for attempting to harm my friend Jacksonia and her family for the sake of love and vengeance. I pray for her health and complete recovery mind, body, soul, and spirit. If Drake or anyone else isn't for me, I ask that you remove them from my space. I have no more to give than I already have. I love you. Thank you for blessing me with

and without. You are everything and I appreciate you and your unconditional love. Amen..."

Chapter 17
Self-Redemption

Sonia submitted the monthly expense report while her coworker Dave gathered receipts. Her phone rang as she began to walk away from her desk.

"This is Jacksonia speaking."

"Hello beautiful." A familiar voice said. How are you feeling?

"I'm doing a lot better Jeffrey!

"I'm happy to hear that. I'm calling to take you out to dinner tonight; if you're free."

"Of course I'll have dinner with you. I forgot you mentioned last week that you will be back in Atlanta today. How are you? How was Chicago?"

"Chicago was great. The artists out there are beyond incredible! What have you been up to since we last spoke?" Jeffrey asked.

"Well, I celebrated what would have been Jaxon's 4th birthday a couple of days ago. It was nothing too major. I decorated my back yard with balloons and a huge teddy bear since he loved being outdoors. I bought a cupcake and lit a candle for him and sent well wishes to heaven."

"Aww love, you didn't have to celebrate alone. I would have flown down sooner to be there with you. I hope you know this."

"I know sweetheart. I actually wanted to be alone. I felt Jaxon's presence the entire time. My baby boy always smiled and loved to love on his Mommy; he and I were all we needed." Sonia told Jeffrey.

"I'm so glad you're back to yourself. I've missed you. I can't wait to see you."

"So am I. The last 8 months without him have been tremendously challenging for me. I'm getting use to my new place. Interior decorating has become a new hobby of mine. Never in a billion years would I have imagined living life without my little man; or his father for Christ sake. However, without prayer, support, and the love of the community, I probably wouldn't have been able to maintain. I remember sitting in bed looking at my caretaker thinking that I couldn't live like that forever. I felt overwhelmed by the accident and I blamed myself every day. I even blamed his father for pissing me off to that degree, but when I think about Terrence I think of how unhealthy our relationship was from the beginning. However, focusing on the things I cannot change has eaten away at my time in the past. So today I solely focus on the things I can control." Sonia said.

"It's awesome to hear you speak so positive about the growth you've made. I'm so proud of you baby." Jeffrey said. "Speaking of Terrence, have you heard from him?"

"I haven't seen or heard from him since the day I lost my baby. The last I discovered, he and his new woman had moved to Texas; and that was only because of the credit card transactions that were made."

"That's really sad there. I could never do that to the mother of my child or the woman I claim to love." Jeffrey told her.

"Every man is unique in their own way. Some happen to be incomparable in certain areas." Sonia said. "I need to get back to work sweetie, but I will see you tonight around 8:30 for dinner."

"Okay beautiful, talk to you soon." Jeffrey said before disconnecting. Sonia left work and walked over to the new women's boutique across the street.

"Hi, welcome to Jovon's!" One of the clerks said.

"Hello. Thank you."

"If there is anything that I can assist you with just let me know. My name is Kelly."

"Thanks Kelly. I'm actually interested in finding a cocktail dress." Sonia told her. "Preferably something black; it's my boyfriend's favorite color."

"You've come to the perfect place for cocktail dresses. Let me direct you in the path of our black pieces. They're just over here." Kelly said stopping to wait on Sonia who suddenly seemed distracted as she looked through the window.

"I'll be right there." Sonia told Kelly as she walked closer to the window. "It can't be!" she said when she noticed Terrence and Karter sitting in the black Jeep Wrangler just outside her new job. It appeared as if they were looking for her. Shortly after Karter jumped behind the wheel while Terrence hopped on the passenger side and they drove away.

"Ma'am." Kelly called.

"Yes. Forgive me. I think I saw an old friend." Sonia told Kelly once she joined her.

"Is everything okay? You seem bewildered." Kelly mentioned. Sonia took a deep breath and clutched her handbag.

"Yes. I'm fine. Let's see what you guys have to offer." Sonia said attempting to act normal. Kelly picked out a few items for her to try on and Sonia made several purchases before heading home. It was around 7:45 pm when she heard a knock on her front door.

"He's here early." Sonia said aloud. She wrapped her wet hair with a towel and slipped on her red satin robe and slippers before heading downstairs to unlock the door. Shouting she said, "Coming!" Sonia unlocked the dead bolt, removed the chain and just as she turned the door knob, the door slammed into her nose. Stunned by what had taken place, she held her bloody nose. Dressed in all black and wearing leather gloves, Terrence, Karter, and the lady from the Bahamas who was voted best at giving head, waltzed into her living room unexpectedly. "Get out of my home! You're not welcomed here!" Sonia screamed.

"You thought you could relocate and I not find you?" Terrence said to Sonia as he gripped her wet hair with one hand and choked her with his other.

"What are you doing here? How did you find me?" Sonia asked trying to breathe and speak at the same time.

"Connections, baby!" Terrence said.

"What do you want Terrence?" Sonia asked as she trembled while trying to avoid falling to the floor by keeping her body balanced. Her erect nipples were peeping through her robe.

"Looks like I still have the magic touch." Terrence spoke sarcastically. "I want three things from you." He continued to say as he sniffed her hair. "First I want an apology from you for sucking another dude's dick." Terrence slung her across the hardwood floor by her hair and Sonia ended up laid out in front of her tile covered fireplace. Her robe had come off revealing her breasts and her black thong. Terrence ran over to her and began pulling her by the neck towards her dining room table. He picked her up and told her to sit in one of the all-white leather rhinestone trimmed seats. Sonia cried and asked him to leave.

"Please just go!" She begged.

"Not so fast baby." Terrence said. He'd pulled out a kitchen axe. Karter and the nameless woman walked over to the table and joined them. The lady tied Sonia's hands and feet in a knot.

"Karter make him stop." Sonia said to him. "We have history. Don't let him do this to me." Karter continued to hide behind his shades without saying a word.

"Now that you're tied down, it's time to slurp on a couple of dicks." Sonia started to squirm as she attempted to get away. Terrence signaled for Karter to get closer to Sonia's mouth. "Go on. Whip your shit out. She's a beast at sucking dick. That pussy may not be worth much, but she won't disappoint with giving head. Karter removed his shades and his gloves and looked down at Sonia prior to pulling his penis out of his pants.

"I'll be gentle." Karter told her. Sonia rolled her eyes and looked away.

"Gentle my ass nigga! Rough that hoe up!" Terrence instructed Karter. Karter held his penis in her face while Terrence forced her mouth wide opened. "Get in there!" Karter finally slid his penis in her mouth and Terrence forcefully moved her head back and forth. She drooled and cried during the whole act. Karter seemed to be somewhat enjoying it, but it was obvious that he wasn't as down as Terrence would have liked for him to be. "Move nigga! Let me show you how it's done!" Terrence said before shoving Karter out of his way. "Open wide bitch!" He said speaking to Sonia. Shoving his penis towards the back of her throat she gagged almost choking. He fucked her face and held her hair firmly around his fingers. Minutes later after humiliating her he ejaculated all over her face and breasts. Sonia continued to cry at the obscene remarks and behavior of her ex. "Journey! Get over here and clean this bitch up!" Sonia immediately looked stunned. Journey walked over to Sonia with a hot wet rag and wiped Terrence's sperm from her body.

"It's you!" Sonia said. "It was you all along!" Journey slightly grinned before speaking.

"I'd do anything to save my family." Journey told Sonia. Sonia looked up at Journey and spit in her face. "You bitch!" Journey said before slapping Sonia.

"I hate you!" I hate all of you!" Sonia screamed piercing their ears. Journey walked over to the sink and grabbed a bucket filled with bloody raw chicken skin and poured it over Sonia's head. Drenched in blood and the heinous odor of spoiled chicken, Sonia kicked and wiggled to the floor. "Get out now!" Sonia demanded. "My neighbors will call the cops!"

"Not so fast, there are two more things that deserve an apology." Terrence said to her. "Take her stink ass upstairs and put her in the bathtub." Terrence instructed Journey and Karter. They picked her up and brought her to the upstairs master bath and put her in the bathtub and ran the water. "Karter let me get that out of your pocket." Terrence said. Karter handed him a bag with a white substance and he put it in Sonia's mouth. "This is a neuromuscular blocking drug that will last for a few hours." Sonia continued to scream for help and cry until she could no longer move anymore.

"Now that I have your undivided attention, I need you to know that I want an apology for removing my name from all of your financial accounts."

"Terrence you've taken everything from me!" Terrence slapped Sonia across her face.

"Bitch did I ask you that?" He shouted. "Apologize!" He demanded.

"Fuck you!" Sonia said. Terrence became extremely frustrated with Sonia and pushed her head under water. Sonia unable to move looked at Terrence with fear in her eyes. Laughing at her immobility Terrence lifted her back up and asked for another apology.

"I'm sorry." Sonia said. "Now please go!"

"Nah, not yet!" Terrence said. He walked over to the bathroom window and opened it wide. "There's one more needed apology you must make!" Terrence handed Karter his cell phone and passed his gloves and sunglasses to Journey. "It's so big; I need to get this on video." He said to Sonia. "You love being on video."

"What are you doing?" Sonia asked crying.

"You'll see!" He told her. "Record me nigga!" Terrence told Karter. Terrence picked Sonia up from the bathtub and dragged her over by her window.

"Karter! You don't have to do this! Make him stop please!" Sonia pleaded. Karter ignored Sonia again and began recording Terrence as he'd requested.

"Last, but certainly not least, apologize for killing my son!" Terrence said to Sonia. Sonia shocked by his proposal looked at Terrence and screamed,

"You killed our son!" Upset and fed up with her hesitating he punched Sonia several times in the face. He looked over at Karter.

"Are you getting this?" Terrence asked as he kicked Sonia in her back and her stomach.

"Stopppppp!" Sonia screamed. "Stop! I apologize!" The bathroom door swung opened and Jeffrey stormed in knocking Karter down with the door and the phone fell from his hand. Journey jumped on Jeffrey's back and he slammed her head into the wall knocking her out cold.

"Leave her alone!" Jeffrey told Terrence.

"You still fuck with this nigga Jeff too?" Terrence asked Sonia. Sonia looked confused at the fact that Terrence knew who Jeffrey was.

"How do you know him?" Sonia mumbled. Terrence giggled.

"Oh he didn't tell you?" Terrence asked grinning. "This is Drake's dude; my decoy nigga." Sonia put her head down in disbelief.

"You set me up too? How dare you!" Sonia told Jeffrey.

"It's not like you think baby!" Jeffrey said.

"Aww isn't this cute. You two can argue another time. I'm in the middle of getting an apology." Terrence told them. He continued to kick Sonia in her stomach.

"That's my baby in there Negro!" Jeffrey revealed to Terrence before slamming him into the open window frame. He helped Sonia from the floor and laid her on her King sized bed. He went back into the bathroom and he and Terrence commenced to brawling. Jeffrey picked Terrence up and slammed him into the mirror over the sink. Glass broke and a piece went into the back of

Terrence's neck. Police sirens were at a distance and Terrence screamed for help. Karter quickly jumped up attempting to help Terrence to their car. Journey still dazed, woke up and followed leaving the gloves, sunglasses, and phone behind.

CHAPTER 18
Poker Face

Sonia was immediately rushed to the hospital to check on the status of her 8 week pregnancy. Jeffrey arrived shortly after to provide the police with Terrence's phone to use as evidence to track him down.

"Baby I'm so happy you and the baby are okay." Jeffrey told Sonia. Sonia looked angrily at Jeffrey.

"Why would you lie to me?" Sonia asked. "I thought we were best friends."

"Baby, I was going to tell you." Jeffrey said.

"When were you going to acknowledge the fact that we met with the help of my husband?"

"Baby I tried telling you. I figured at this point it didn't matter." Jeffrey said.

"Why wouldn't it matter Jeffrey? Is our relationship not that significant for you to let me know what's going on?"

"You just said Terrence is your husband. I can't compete with a man who can call my woman his wife. Get a divorce and then expect more from me." Jeffrey said out of frustration.

"Listen! I've explained several times that I can't divorce him if I do not know where he is to serve him with divorce papers. I don't love him anymore. My heart is with you and our unborn child." Sonia told him. "Now when you're ready, I'd like to know when the two of you first met.

"Okay, well this is what happened. The fellas gathered at your place on a Sunday evening for poker. He invited my home boy Drake, his neighbors Hugo, Todd and Eric, his co- worker Harold, and I came along with Drake. You'd prepared a quick snack for us before heading over to your home girl Syn's place. We drank beer and liquor and smoked cigars all while playing Texas Hold'em. Everything seemed to be going well until Terrence and Drake began discussing untrustworthy women."

'Yeah my woman was there for me during the time I was on Chemo and recovering from my illness, but I still don't completely trust her.' Terrence stated.

'Then why the hell are you marrying her within the next six months, Bro?' Drake asked him.

'Drake, homie, my ninja, I can't do it just yet.' Drake and the rest of the guys looked confused.

Terrence began to explain his case. 'I'm currently seeking a decoy.'

'A decoy?' Todd shouted.

'Yes a decoy.' Terrence reiterated.

'Isn't that some shit the ladies attempt to use when trying to setup their lover?' Harold asked.

'That's exactly what it is Harold.' Terrence said.

'Boy you are foolish.' Drake told him.

'Listen, I have to know before I get locked into some shit for the rest of my life.'

'I don't blame you.' Eric told Terrence. 'My wife is not the same woman I proposed to.' He added.

'So what's the plan?' Drake asked.

'The plan is to see if the pussy is really mine.' Terrence looked over at me trying to piece me up. 'What about you? What's your story?' Terrence asked me. I smiled in a blushful manner.

'I don't have a story.' I responded.

'Everyone has a story.' Terrence told me. I sighed before speaking.

'I'm newly separated, no kids, own a couple of businesses, God- fearing, and as hardworking as they come.' I revealed.

'You'll be perfect.' Terrence told me. He looked at Drake trying to get him to encourage me to participate in his charade.

'I'm not really into things like that.' I added.

'It could be fun, Jeff. If you don't get the ass at least you would have put a smile on her face. Something this fool hasn't done in a while.' Drake said sarcastically.

'Man I take real good care of my woman. I just need to be certain that she's the perfect woman she portrays to be.' Terrence shared.

'Okay.' I agreed.

'Okay what?' Drake asked me.

'Okay, I'll do it.' I said to Drake.

'Good.' Terrence said. 'I like this fella Drake.' Terrence and I exchanged information before departing for the evening. Drake dapped up Terrence before leaving out the door.

'Your boy legit?' Terrence asked him.

'Definitely.' Drake assured him.

"And that's how it went down." Jeffrey explained to Sonia.

"I can't believe this. First Terrence sets me up, then Syn, now you. How could you all betray me like this? I don't understand." Sonia said.

"Baby, I'm not here to hurt you. I'm sorry if it seems as if I don't care about you, but I do. I love all of you. You're beautiful inside and out. You're everything I need in a woman and more. You have to just trust in me." Jeffrey said to her. He kissed her on her forehead, covered her with a blanket and laid in bed next to her. Not too long after drifting off to sleep, a detective knocked on the door and asked if he could have a moment to speak with Sonia. Jeffrey got up and left them in private.

"Hi Mrs. Coleman, I'm Detective Larson."

"Please call me Sonia."

"According to the video footage we retrieved, Mr. Coleman wanted to harm you and your child."

"Yes detective; that is correct. I'm not sure if he was aware of my pregnancy or not, but Jeffrey, my boyfriend, informed him."

"I see." The detective said. "I came to let you know that his real name isn't Terrence. It's Ethan Allen. He and his wife Serenity Bryant aka Journey Kerry have made a career out of fabricating their identities." He informed Sonia.

"Wow! Are you being serious right now?" Sonia asked. "I've known him since college! I can't believe it! I'm overwhelmed!" Sonia added.

"I'm sure you are. The high school sweethearts both grew up as foster kids. They fell in love and got married just out of high school." Detective Larson showed Sonia photos of them as well as a copy of their marriage license.

"Oh my God! What does this mean for our marriage?" Sonia asked.

"It means that your marriage is null and void. You will have to fax over some important annulment documents, and once those are submitted, you will be considered single again. In the meantime, I would suggest that you get new credit cards and put a security alert on all of your accounts. With the assistance of your boyfriend Jeffrey, it seems as if we've linked Karter Charles aka King Karter as a relative of Ethan. We are already building a case against him and well that will make it easier to locate their whereabouts." Sonia sat up in bed with mixed emotions.

"I'm happy we're able to help."